The War That Changed My Life

Lianne Smith

Copyright © Lianne Smith 2012

Cover Artist: Lianne Smith

Editor: Lianne Smith

Printed in the United Kingdom

First Printing, 2012

Published by Lulu.com

ISBN 978-1-4717-9612-8

I dedicate this book to my family, without them I would not have been able to achieve any of this.

Chapter One

Present Day

Lying on my back every day was beginning to get annoying and there wasn't anything I could do about it. I had been admitted into hospital with pneumonia a few weeks beforehand and while the doctors hadn't told me what was going on, I could tell they weren't sure how long I was going to last. It was all evident in their sympathetic smiles, their kind eyes, the cautious words. I used to be the same when I was a nurse and it was quite infuriating.

I was 88 years old. I had survived a war, I had survived giving birth to two children and had survived being surrounded by several boisterous grandchildren, yet it appeared that a little case of pneumonia was going to kill me. I would have been comical had it not been so tragically true.

I groaned in agony as a cough wracked my body and was immediately surrounded by my daughters and their children. I had the pleasure of being visited by my entire family since they'd decided to surprise me as a group, but it did mean that I had to sit through arguments about who sat where for the first 10 minutes of their visit. My daughters sat either side of me and kept a hold of both of my hands. I looked over and gave them both a pained smile, it was incredible how much like their father they looked – a fact that I had found fairly painful since his death.

"Grammy, are you okay?" My youngest granddaughter, Suzie, asked me with a tight voice, her deep blue eyes were wide in worry. I hated that they had to see me like this but they weren't prepared to leave my side in case I died without them there. I wasn't planning on it though; I still had some fight left in me. I just wanted to get out of the blasted bed.

"Fine, I'm fine." I smiled and stretched out to stroke her pale blonde hair in reassurance. She moved from the foot of the bed and perched herself on her mother's knees.

My eldest daughter, Betty, started fussing with the pillows behind my head. "I'm fine darling, you needn't worry." I sighed when she didn't listen to me.

"I just want you to be comfortable ma; I don't want you to get a crick in the neck." She glanced down at me and gave me a warm smile. "It's the least I can do since you're stuck in here."

"A crick in the neck is the least of my worries!" I grumbled and wiggled around a little until I was sitting up slightly, able to see the rest of the familiar faces. I never seemed to be comfortable for more than a few minutes in this bed; it made me sorely miss the lumpy mattress that I had back at the care home.

"What did you say?" She watched my face and sat back down.

"I said that I'll be all right; I'm just fed up of lying down in this blooming bed!" I moaned in annoyance.

Elsie, my other daughter, laughed a little. "You're never happy are you ma? When you're up you want to lie down and when you're down you want to get up!" I couldn't see her face since Suzie was sat on her knee, but I could tell she was sticking her tongue out. I rolled my eyes.

"You'd be the same if you had the body of a 90 year old!"

They both laughed at me. "We're nearly there!"

"Not likely, 30 years is a long way to go."

There was a short silence throughout the room, my grandchildren moved around until they were all perched on the bed instead of standing around. Elsie glanced over at them and then looked back at me with a small smile.

"Ma, why don't you tell us a story or something and try to take your mind off the fact you aren't comfortable?" Elsie suggested with a small shrug and a sheepish smile.

"Haven't you girls heard everything I've had to say, several times?"

"Well we haven't!" Stevie, my youngest grandson, exclaimed. "You never tell us anything anymore nanny! Tell us something!"

I sighed, "What do you want to hear?"

"Why don't you tell them about the war?" Elsie suggested. I shook my head.

"Really? Why? It's just an old lady's memory about something that happened 70 years ago. They won't want to hear about it."

"We do actually; I've been meaning to ask you about the war." Suzie added with a bright smile and a quick wink in Elsie's direction. I narrowed my eyes at the both of them.

"I don't know…" I muttered. "It's quite painful to recall…"

"Ma, just tell them." Betty said.

I looked around the room and sighed at the faces staring back at me in expectation. "I'm not going to be able to remember everything; things get a little fuzzy with old age you know!"

"Then tell them how you met Dad?" Betty shrugged and leant back in her chair, I watched as she also winked at Elsie.

"Why do they want to know about that?"

Suzie looked between the three of us and then cleared her throat. "Because from the bits and pieces I've heard, it's rather romantic and on top of that, you were working during the war! I've always wanted to know what it was like."

"But…" I tried to come up with another excuse but fell blank, I'd never told the story fully before, not even to my two daughters because some parts were just too painful to remember. I was pretty sure that they weren't going to accept the usual spiel I gave, so with a defeated sigh, I began to tell them everything from a life that was long forgotten.

***

It was all they talked about – getting ready for war – but it soon became apparent that it was all talk and no action. The real shock hit the country when Prime Minister Neville Chamberlain made the announcement on Sunday 3rd September 1939. On an otherwise cheery day, a sombre tone hit England as his voice reverberated out of radios all over the country, filling rooms with the sad news.

'I am speaking to you from the Cabinet Room at 10 Downing Street.'

Families stopped what they were doing as the Prime Minister continued speaking. Nothing was more important at that moment than knowing what was about to happen.

'This morning the British Ambassador in Berlin handed the German Government a final note stating that, unless we hear from them by 11 o'clock that they were prepared at once to withdraw their troops from Poland, a state of war would exist between us.'

It was the next words that changed that day for everyone.

'I have to tell you that no such undertaking has been received and that consequently this country is at war with Germany.'

I was only 18 when the war started and was in no way prepared for how it completely changed my life.

****

Chapter Two

1939

Within minutes of the finished radio broadcast an eerie silence fell on the area of Swiss Cottage, this was it – the country was at war.

My mamma, a plump woman in her early forties, made her way into the garden to look up at the sky. "But it's such a nice day!" She whispered as if it was going to change anything. She was right; it was a surprisingly nice day, especially for the time of year. The sun was out, the birds were singing but everything already felt different.

"Don't you worry Beth; it'll be over by Christmas." My father spoke as he took her into his arms to calm her down.

"How can you be so sure Robert? How can you be so sure?" she wailed before burying her face in his chest and shaking her head vigorously. My baby twin brothers, Michael and David, didn't quite understand what had happened and why mamma was so upset.

"What's wrong with mamma?" Michael asked after he had been tugging on my father's trousers for a while.

"The war, son." He smiled sadly down at the both of them; they still looked just as confused.

"What's a war?" David innocently questioned, father sighed.

"I'll tell you when you're older."

I smiled softly. That was the old 'get-out' clause. Father would always say that to us if the conversation when on to a subject that he didn't like, or didn't want us to know about.

John, my elder brother, frowned. "The war is a fight to the death between us and the bloody Jerrys!" he spat as he kicked the ground in disgust.

"John!" Mamma reprimanded. Father gave him a stern look and shook his head disapprovingly. "We didn't want them to worry John, you needn't have said anything."

Father gently pushed mamma away from him and grabbed his son by the cuff of the ear before dragging him into the house. I didn't need to hear the yelps of pain to know that he was getting the slipper. I walked up to mamma and put an arm around her shoulders.

She focused her teary eyes on me. "Rose, you know what this means don't you?"

I did, I was just as upset as she was. "Your father, John, my brother – everybody – they'll need them for the war…" she took in a shaky breath.

"I know mamma, but without their help we won't win." I leant my head on her shoulder and looked up at the sky. She kissed my hair and sighed again. "I'm just scared."

***

Although the day of the announcement felt different and we were suddenly very much on edge, nothing else changed. We were all prepared for the invasion we'd been assured was imminent. We'd been meticulously told how to put up our blackout curtains and how to make sure that there wasn't even the tiniest sliver of light showing, we'd been reminded that careless talk cost lives and that we had to keep our gas masks with us at all times. Yet, nothing happened.

Pamphlets were posted through our doors every day, sometimes more than once, air raid sirens would go off at all hours to allow for practice and our neighbours started to erect Anderson shelters that had been given out earlier in the year in case of a suspected bombing. We were all poised and ready for action, but there was none.

Slowly, as if coming out of a deep hazy sleep, everybody's lives went back to normal. Our daily routine returned and everybody seemed to relax again. There were only little things that changed throughout the months ending 1939 but even then it wasn't anything massively important for us to really acknowledge the war that seemed to be happening on the other side of the world.

In October the government called for men between the ages of 20 and 23 to fight for their country, they left soon after. For a while it was weird not having my brother or my cousins around but it soon became normality and we just accepted that they'd be back soon. Mamma had attempted to evacuate Michael and David throughout October, shipping them off to family that lived in the country but every time she said goodbye to them at the train station, she very quickly changed her mind.

"I can't leave my babies on their own!" she once explained to me. "I'd much rather they stayed with me in London than be with family that they've never met. No matter how nice Aunty Vera is!"

It wouldn't have mattered if she'd managed to send them away; by the time we reached December most of the children had made their way home again.

***

"Rose?" mamma called out one morning. I was in the pantry helping her sift through the potatoes we'd bough in from our allotment.

"Yes mamma?" I stepped out into the kitchen and waited for her to enter. She trotted in, her face flushed and her hair sticking out of her bandana at all angles. "The children are back!"

I raised an eyebrow before frowning, "What do you mean?"

She beckoned me to follow her and went trotting back into the sitting room by the window. When I caught up with her and looked outside I saw that the neighbourhood children were back in the street, playing the games they'd played months before.

"Must mean the war is nearly over if they're sending the children back. Your daddy was right; it will be over by Christmas." Mamma gushed as she clapped her hands together happily. I put my arm around her waist and leant against her shoulder, I really hoped for her sake that she was right.

The sunny evenings turned into blisteringly cold nights. Air raids were becoming more frequent but since it was just too cold to go out to the Anderson shelter my father had arranged, we ended up staying in bed. We knew nothing was going to happen, there wasn't any threat.

In fact, the only time that the threat of war seemed real was December 22nd 1939. We'd run out of the front door when we heard the steady fall of feet and for a fleeting moment had thought that our families were home. Instead we stood watching a group of about fifty Canadian soldiers marching the streets of London. They were all wearing the same green outfit, a shirt with double breast plates, trousers that had two different sized pockets and were all walking in unison. It was such an incredibly amazing thing to watch these soldiers march forcefully but gracefully through the area.

After a short while mamma's face fell.

"Mamma?" I called softly. She looked over at me with tears in her eyes.

"I thought they'd be back by now. I had everything sorted."

I sighed sadly, although everybody thought the war would have been over by now, none of our men had come back. We didn't know exactly what was going on, but we knew enough to know that it wasn't over. "They'll be home soon. Just you wait." I smiled encouragingly before turning back to the march and watching in awe as they moved past.

"Mamma! Who are they?" Michael asked quietly, breaking the silence that had drifted between us.

"Canadian soldiers dear." She replied with a sad smile. He nodded and kept quiet for a little while.

"What's a Canadium?" Mamma laughed a little, her earlier tears forgotten as she took in the confused face of her baby.

"Canadian darling, not Canadium. They're people from another country in the world."

Michael continued to look confused for a short while. "Why are they here?"

She shrugged and picked him up, "I have no idea darling. They must be here to help us."

I glanced down at David who was tugging on the bottom of my dress. "Rose, up!" he lifted his arms in the air – for a three year old, he wasn't very talkative. I picked him up and held him on my hip, pointing out the different waves of soldiers and the different posts between them.

"Mamma, have you heard from father?" I asked when the boys had run off into the street with the other children and had started to imitate the soldiers. She nodded slowly.

"It was brief; he just wanted to let us know that they were all safe and should be back on leave soon."

I smiled, "Do you know where they are?"

Mamma shook her head, "they can't tell us that sweetheart in case the letters get intercepted or something. I'm just glad to know that they're all okay."

***

The novelty of seeing the Canadian soldiers soon wore off, the march subsided and everyone went back into their houses to carry on with what they'd been doing before the interruption. I didn't think much of the soldiers until later that evening when one of my friends from school came knocking.

"Is Rose in?" they asked mamma, who nodded and stepped aside to let them in.

"Rose darling, you have a friend here to see you." Mamma called up the stairs. I put the book I was reading on the table and trotted downstairs. "Joan!" I exclaimed as I reached the bottom, we'd not seen each other since August when she joined the nurses' station a town over.

"Rose! How are you?"

I grinned, "I'm good thank you. How are you? How is it being a nurse?" She then grinned at me and took my arm before dragging me back up to my room and telling me about her adventures.

"It's so weird!" she exclaimed happily. "I feel so useful but useless at the same time."

"What do you mean?" I asked.

"Well, I'll be here when the wounded come in, but I can't do anything until then. I'm still in training…"

I nodded slowly and glanced down at my hands with a fearful smile.

"Do you think we'll get wounded then?" I asked quietly. Joan shrugged and patted my hand.

"I don't know, but I want to be there in case we do…" She smiled sympathetically and put an arm around my shoulder.

"Your brother and your cousins are going to be fine. In fact they're probably all sat around a table playing cards as we speak."

I smiled gratefully at her attempt to cheer me up. "I suppose you're right. Everything is going to be fine."

We continued chatting about what had happened over the last couple of months, catching each other up with any gossip that we'd missed during our time apart. We hadn't realised just how late it was getting until mamma came in and asked Joan to leave since the boys were in bed.

"Joan, darling, it's getting late and the boys are in bed. Perhaps you can carry this conversation on tomorrow?" Mamma had asked with a polite smile and a small blush, she hated having to ask people to go. I took Joan downstairs and passed her the coat she'd left on the banister.

"Have a safe journey. Please be careful, you have no idea where the cars are in this blackout." I frowned a little in worry, the number of roadside accidents involving people and other vehicles had dramatically increased since we'd started having blackouts every night. Car headlights were covered; they were only allowed to have one thin beam showing which made walking anywhere during the night extremely dangerous.

She gave me a smile and another reassuring pat on the hand, "Oh, don't worry. I'm staying with Aunt Bertha and she's near the fields."

I turned to open the door when she caught my arm again. "Before I forget, did you see those soldiers earlier?"

I nodded, "How could anybody have missed them? There were so many!" Joan smiled slightly and then blushed for a reason unbeknownst to me.

"Well, the school is hosting its annual Christmas Eve 'Eve' party tomorrow and I've been informed that those soldiers are going."

I gasped and then clamped a hand over my mouth in case I'd been too noisy. "Really?"

"Yes. Please come? You've not been to one for years!"

"I don't know..."

"Rose, the last time you went to one we were 14, that's four years! Please come?"

I sighed, "But mamma..."

I hadn't heard mamma walk downstairs and jumped and she spoke over me.

"Mamma thinks it's a good idea. You need to go out and have some fun Rose."

I went to argue that I didn't want to leave her on her own but she raised a hand to quieten my protests.

"I'll be fine; Victoria is supposed to be popping around anyway."

"But..." I went to protest again, part of me really didn't want to go to the party yet it was overruled majorly by both Joan and mamma. Though, I did have a slightly curiosity about the soldiers.

"Fine." I conceded. Joan squealed and threw her arms around me.

"We're going to have so much fun!"

I smiled and waved to her as she left the house. Mamma put her arm around my shoulders, squeezed me to her before kissing the top of my head and walking us into the sitting room.

****

Chapter Three

I stood outside my old school shuffling around on my feet.

"Would you please calm down?" Joan hissed as she drew her coat closer around her. The weather had taken a decidedly colder turn and waiting around in a dress wasn't the best idea.

"I am calm!" I hissed back at her before I started bouncing around on my feet. I wasn't calm, I was extremely nervous - I hadn't been to the school since I'd left it two years ago and I really wasn't great with social interaction.

"Why are you bouncing around then?" she asked in annoyance. I sighed and stopped myself from moving for long enough so she turned away and carried on chatting to the person in front of me.

***

"I really don't want to be here!" I cried when we walked into the hall that had been decorated for the dance.

"Please stop complaining, I want to enjoy myself tonight!"

I rolled my eyes, "Okay, you're right. I'm sorry." I smiled apologetically and then let Joan know that I was going to find myself somewhere to sit. She didn't seem too happy that I was going to hide away at the side of the room but begrudgingly understood that I wasn't comfortable.

"I'll come over and talk to you in a little while, 'kay?" she said with a smile before greeting a couple of other people. I walked away with a nod and found myself a dark little corner of the room where I could keep an eye on Joan and watch what was going on at the same time.

I glanced over at the door when the room fell silent and watched as the soldiers walked in. They were chatting and laughing together until they realised that everybody was looking at them. It was quite comical to watch as there were two groups of people staring at each other with a vast space between them, though the conversations started up again after a couple of minutes. I looked over at what the soldiers were wearing and was pleasantly surprised when I noticed they weren't in their uniform but had managed to come wearing suits.

The music started not long after they entered and I realised immediately that it was completely different to what I was used to. It was much livelier and bouncier than the music we listened to and apparently was much more fun to dance to, if the glee on the girls' faces was anything to go by.

With a defeated sigh I moved from my corner and perched on a chair that had recently become unoccupied and watched the various couples dancing around the room.

"Dances not your thing?"

I jumped a little when I heard the voice and turned to face them. I was a little surprised to be looking directly into the eyes of one of the Canadian soldiers. He gave me a wide smile which caused me to blush.

"I…err…No?" I stammered and shook my head at the same time. The grin never slid off of his face.

"The name's Edward." He thrust his hand in front of me and waited for a few seconds, when I made no move he raised an eyebrow and lowered his hand slowly.

"What's yours darling?"

I opened my mouth a couple of times before I managed to speak again. "Rose."

"That's a pretty name." He winked at me. "Maybe I'll see you around Rose." He stood with a brief smile and quickly made his way back over to a group of soldiers that had been watching us. I stared after him in complete wonderment and inwardly groaned at my lack of poise. Joan flitted over with a look of shock on her face.

"How do you do that!?" she asked quickly and glanced around the room.

"Do what?" I questioned.

"Sit there, look miserable and still get the best looking guy?" she laughed a little. "He came over to talk to me but you caught his eye and off he went."

"It doesn't mean anything really; we didn't actually talk about much." I mentioned.

"But he was constantly smiling! What did you talk about then?" She asked in disbelief before glancing down at her shoe and frowning.

"He asked me my name…" I shrugged.

"And…?"

"That's it. He got my name and then left."

"Surely she said something more to you?" she asked, I shook my head.

"No. he asked me what my name was, I told him and he said" I coughed so I could lower my voice "That's a nice name. Maybe

I'll see you around Rose.'" I shrugged. "What am I supposed to say to that?"

Joan giggled and rolled her eyes, "You're impossible. Rose, go find him and talk to him. He's gorgeous."

I shook my head, "I couldn't, I'm too nervous."

"Rose! You only live once…"

"I don't care and I just want to go home." I grumbled. Joan put her beaker on the floor and turned to face me.

"How many dances have you been to in the last four years?"

"None…"

"How many men have started chatting to you that you didn't know?"

"None…"

"Exactly! Now go and find him and chat, what's the worst thing that could happen?"

I didn't answer her and she smiled. "There you go, now find him before I do because I won't let him go if I get the chance!"

She jumped up and walked back over to a group of our friends, leaving me sat on the chair with a terrified look on my face and panic arising in my stomach. If mamma had let me stay at home, I wouldn't be in this situation, instead I'd be happily at the house fixing whatever clothes the boys had ripped and I would be making sure she was all right.

***

After giving myself a rather lengthy pep talk, I stood up and wandered over to the punch table to get myself a drink.

"Oh, so she moves!" A voice behind me laughed as they steadied my shaking hand. I glanced behind me to see who it was and smiled when I saw Edward. I scowled playfully at him.

"Wo-ah, easy tiger! I was just joking."

I turned around so my back was to the table and faced him. I sipped at my drink and watched as he seemed to have an internal argument with himself, his mouth had opened several times but he'd frowned before he said anything and then had tried again. I raised an amused eyebrow and smiled softly in encouragement.

"Would you care to dance?" he asked nervously as he took the drink from my hand. I nodded slowly and very cautiously followed him onto the dance floor. He wound one arm around my waist and very gently took my other hand as we started to dance.

"Are you usually this quiet?" he mused after I again hadn't said anything for a few minutes.

"Not usually, no." I mumbled out, blushing when I watched him smile. He was so gorgeous that it was making me nervous, much more nervous than I was usually. He had broad shoulders, a shock of dark hair and lovely green eyes that were set perfectly in his muscular face just above an aquiline nose.

"Why are you so quiet now then?" He asked softly and drew me a tiny bit closer as the song slowed down.

"I'm very shy…"I whispered and carried on the mental appreciation of the Canadian I was dancing with.

"I've noticed." He laughed heartily and then spun me away from him before pulling me back and swaying us to the music again.

"Why are you here if you're shy and dances aren't your thing?" He questioned just before the song finished.

"My mamma and my friend forced me to come." I explained with a sideways glance at Joan who was looking at me with a severe case of jealousy. I stuck my tongue out at her and grinned when she through her hands up in despair.

"What's so funny?" Edward asked softly as we turned to leave the dance floor. I smiled up at him.

"I was just winding a friend up."

He chuckled, "Was it *the* friend?" I nodded. He smirked, looked over his shoulder and saw Joan who was still watching us. He waved and threw her a smile, which caused her to blush, before turning his attention back to me and taking my hand to walk us back to the corner where we'd met.

"Thank you for the dance." Edward smiled and went to leave but I stopped him before he had the chance.

"Would you like to go outside and get some fresh air?" I asked quickly, a little surprised at my confidence. Edward also looked slightly shocked.

"Oh! Yes, that would be nice." He grinned and then looked around the room. "I just need to go and grab my jacket; I'll be back in a moment." He held one hand up to tell me to wait for a second and dashed out of the room to grab his coat. He returned in less than a minute and held out his arm for me to take. I linked mine through his and let him lead me to the doors that took us outside. We stopped briefly to figure out where to go and then spotted somewhere we could go and talk quietly without being completely hidden.

We made our way over to the little fountain we'd seen and sat down on one of the benches that had been placed around it. Edward and I sat in silence for a while, just watching each other.

"Forgive me for being forward, but you're incredibly beautiful."

He muttered quietly and then glanced down at the floor as he blushed. I smiled at him.

"Thank you." I laughed a little, "You're not so bad yourself."

He looked a little shocked at what I'd said but grinned at me.

"Sense of humour. I like that."

I shivered and wrapped my arms around myself to try and keep me warm. Edward watched and then took his coat off and gently placed it on my shoulders.

"Here, I don't need it." He wrapped it around me and smoothed down the arms before dropping his hands back into his lap and looking at me shyly. "Better now?"

I nodded, "Much, thank you." I grabbed the collar of the coat and brought it up to my nose under the pretence of keeping my face warm, instead I breathed in his smell.

"I'm glad you decided to turn up tonight ya know Rose. You may be uncomfortable but you've made my night."

I laughed a little, "You've barely spoken to me."

He shrugged, "Well, not as such, but I already know that you're more interesting than those girls in there." He smiled and brushed a stray piece of hair away from my face. "You may be quiet but you're friendly, you have a sense of humour and you're not staring at us like we're weird or something."

"They're just not used to new people." I explained with a half-hearted smile. "Especially soldiers from another country."

Edward smiled wryly and shuffled around a little, "I hate this war." He muttered.

"Well, you're quiet safe here in England, nothing is happening." I told him with a bright smile. The sad look on his face didn't change though.

"I wouldn't convince yourself of that darlin', you don't know what's going on just over the ocean." He bit his lip and shook his head.

"What is going on?" I asked slowly.

"I'm sorry; I can't tell you that Rose. Military confidentiality, we don't know who could be listening over us."

I nodded my head in understanding and tried to think of something that we could instead talk about.

"Tell me about yourself Rose." Edward said.

I bit my lip in concentration. "What do you want to know?"

"Anything that you're willing to share, I just want to get to know you."

I smiled softly, "Well, only if you tell me about yourself afterwards."

Edward grinned, "Deal."

***

We stayed talking outside until Joan came out to look for me. She scowled when she saw that I was with Edward but otherwise informed me that the dance was slowing down and that we should get ready to leave.

"When can I see you again?" Edward stopped me as I was about to walk into the hall.

"When do you leave?" I questioned and wondered if he could actually divulge that information.

"Not for a few weeks yet…" he smiled a little and clasped his hands together in front of him.

"Tomorrow?" I asked without thinking, it then dawned on me that it was Christmas Eve. Which a frustrated sigh, I retracted my offer. "Actually, tomorrow isn't so good; I have to help mamma with the Christmas dinner."

Edward smiled, "I could help you? I used to love helping my mam when I was younger."

I nodded enthusiastically, "That would be lovely." I waved goodbye, walked into the hall, quickly spotted Joan and made my way over to her.

"Wait! Rose!" Edward called after me. He ran into the room and quickly caught up with me.

"Where do you live?" he asked with a brief laugh. I blushed.

"I was testing you…" I tried to cover my forgetfulness, "I live down the road at-"

"Wait. Is it just you and your friend walking home?" he questioned with a frown. I nodded.

"No male supervision?"

"Nope, nobody is here for us to have that..."

"Right, well I'll walk you home then. That way I'll know where you live and you'll be safe!" He grinned at his idea and put his arm around my shoulders.

"That would be lovely." I said with a smile and shivered as he pulled me into his side. Joan walked over with a bemused smile and handed me my coat.

"Ready to leave?" she asked whilst quickly glancing at Edward.

"He's walking us back to mine Joanie, so we're safe." I told her with a massive grin. She nodded and started to walk ahead of us. We followed her in silence and tried to keep up with her as she stormed off. I had no idea what was bothering her but I was surely going to find out in the morning. I shuddered as I felt Edward's hand clasp mine and glanced up at him.

"Is this okay?" he asked quietly. I nodded and smiled.

We were half way home when I realised that I was still wearing his coat and that he seemed to be shivering.

"Oh! I'm so sorry! Would you like your coat back?" I went to take it off and put mine on but he shook his head and stopped me.

"No, you keep it warm. I'll take it back when you're home safely."

"Aren't you cold?" I questioned in concern.

"Freezing," he replied with a laugh and then shook his head when I started to take his coat off again. "Seriously, keep it. I've been colder."

With a defeated sigh I kept his coat around my shoulders but moved closer to him and kept his hand in his coat pocket with mine. He smiled gratefully at my efforts to warm him up.

***

I waved goodbye to Joan and Edward when we got to the house and snuck inside as quietly as possible. The living room light turned on, making me jump whilst illuminating the dark room with a sliver of light.

"It's quite late..." Mamma mumbled through a yawn. I immediately felt guilty.

"I'm sorry; I guess time just got away from me." I walked into the living room and perched on the edge of the arm chair with a small smile. Mamma looked at me oddly for a few seconds and started frowning.

"Whose coat is that?"

I glanced down and gasped. I'd forgotten to give Edward his coat back again.

"Oh! It's Edward's! He must be frozen..." I jumped up and ran to the front door.

"Where are you going?" Mamma asked with a bemused smile.

"I need to give it back to him, he was only lending it to me because I was cold and it's freezing outside." I smiled at her before opening the door and trotting out. Thankfully Edward was still waiting at the bottom of the steps. He laughed and took his coat gratefully.

"Thank goodness you realised eh? I would've caught pneumonia otherwise!"

I smiled apologetically, "I hadn't realised. It was mamma, if she hadn't noticed I doubt you'd have gotten it back."

"I was going to knock but I remembered you said you had younger brothers and I didn't want to wake them."

"It's all right, they sleep like logs usually." I turned to go back into the house but Edward caught my hand.

"Thank you for a really nice night." He grinned at me and pulled me into him for a hug. "It has been great!"

I stumbled away from him and giggled hysterically before I waved goodbye again and ran back into the house. Mamma had moved from her spot on the chair and was standing near the door.

"Is that Edward?" she whispered whilst I closed the door after I'd thrown him another smile.

"Yeah, he's one of the Canadian soldiers." I explained through a happy sigh and leant against the door with a grin on my face. "He's lovely."

"Did you meet him tonight?" she asked slowly. I nodded and watched her to see if she was annoyed, instead she winked and put her arm around my shoulders.

"Why don't we go and sit in the kitchen, listen to the wireless and you can tell me about your night?" she suggested. I glanced over at her with concern.

"Aren't you tired?"

She shook her head and gave me another smile. "Not tonight. Tonight I want to hear about everything that happened."

I laughed and sat down at the kitchen table whilst she turned the wireless on and sorted out the kettle.

"Well, not much really happened if I'm particularly honest…I didn't really want to go." I mumbled and looked down at my hands on the table.

"Why didn't you want to go?" she looked surprised as she asked me this. I wasn't entirely sure why though; I'd made it clear that I wasn't happy going.

"I'd have preferred to stay home with you and the boys." I shrugged in indifference and started to listen to the song on the wireless. The room fell silent as mamma fixed us both some tea and set the steaming cups in front of us.

"You wouldn't have met Edward if you didn't go." She retorted. I tried to suppress a smile at the mention of Edward's name but she caught me out. She laughed a little and shook her head in amusement.

"Right, tell me how you met him…"

I rolled my eyes, laughed and then started to tell her about how he'd come over to me and had started to talk to me, albeit very briefly, but he spoke first nonetheless. Mamma didn't say anything until I'd finished talking; she just kept nodding and smiling.

"Ooh, it's all very romantic isn't it?" she laughed and picked up our cups to wash them. I followed her so I could dry them.

"When does he leave?" Mamma asked with a small frown. I shrugged.

"He didn't specify, he just told me it was in a few weeks."

"Does he have any family in London?" she asked me slowly. I cast my mind back to the conversation by the fountain as I tried to remember if he'd mentioned it.

"I…don't think so."

"So, what is doing over Christmas?"

"Oh! He wanted to come over and help us cook dinner tomorrow."

Mamma looked at me with a huge grin on her face. "Well, that saves me asking to get him to come over. He'll spend Christmas with us; it'll be nice to have a man around the house again."

I smiled sympathetically and rubbed her arm. My father leaving for war had hit her rather hard and I knew that she hated being without him, even if she tried to hide it.

****

Chapter Four

I was awoken by the butterflies that had taken up residence in my stomach. It was Christmas Eve, which I loved enough on its own, but Edward was coming over to join us too which made it all the more exciting. I bounded down the stairs and trotted into the kitchen with a massive grin on my face.

"Somebody is happy!" Mamma mused as she flitted about with the boys breakfast while they were sitting at the table playing with little rocks they'd found.

"Who happy?" Michael asked with wide eyes as he looked between mamma and me. I grinned at me, picked him up and spun him around, enjoying the little peals of laughter he was emitting.

"I am, sunshine!"

He giggled, nuzzled his head into the side of my face and wound his tiny arms around my neck. "Again! Again!" he squealed in delight as I continued spinning him around. After a little while I flopped onto a seat barely able to see steadily in front of me. He let go and perched on my lap, his little face a peculiar shade of green.

"Dizzy…" he mumbled sadly and shook his head to clear the fuzziness, I laughed in agreement. I was incredibly dizzy too.

"Rose, what time is Edward coming over?" Mamma asked when she'd put the boys breakfast down on the table. I turned to face her and blinked a couple of times to clear my vision.

"I'm not entirely sure…early afternoon I think."

She nodded and sat down on the other seat. "Did you arrange a time?"

I bit my lip and thought back to the previous night before shaking my head slowly. "No…I don't think so…"

Mamma laughed, "Well, that's extremely helpful. He won't be over early will he?"

I shrugged and put Michael on the floor with his piece of bread. "I doubt it; he knows that the boys are little. I'll go and get dressed in case though." I smiled at mamma, "If he turns up earlier than expected, I'll get him into the living room so you can go upstairs without being seen in your nightdress."

Mamma smiled thankfully as I raced out of the kitchen and took the stairs two at a time.

***

Edward didn't come to the house until mid-afternoon in the end. I would've been lying if I said that I hadn't sat near the front window and watched impatiently for him to turn up, for the majority of the morning. Mamma kept catching me staring out of the window and was finding the entire situation quite amusing.

"You're being silly Rose; he'll get here when he gets here." She rolled her eyes when she saw me plastered against the window.

"I know, but I want to see when does get here. So I can be prepared."

"Prepared for what?"

"Prepared for the fact that a boy I like will be in the house." I told her in one breath.

Mamma shook her head with a laugh and wandered back into the kitchen, humming along with the wireless as she went. My heart leapt into my throat and started racing when I watched him walk up the path from the garden gate.

I squeaked and jumped off of the sofa, falling to the ground in a heap. My legs had tangled in a blanket that I'd knocked onto the floor. I heard mamma laugh in the kitchen as I stood up.

"He's here then?"

I rolled my eyes, walked to the door and patted down my skirt a few times before I was happy I didn't look a mess. I opened the door with a brilliant smile on my face.

"Hello!" I chirped and stepped aside to let him come in. "Found the house all right in the daylight then?" I asked with a smile and took his coat from him so I could hang it up. He gave me a quick one armed hug and then nodded.

"I thought I was staying a lot further away than I actually am. I'm just down the road really." He smiled at me and then chuckled. He reached out and pushed a loose strand of hair behind my ear.

"Oh! Are you staying at the Horse and Hound?" I squeaked whilst blushing before leading him into the kitchen.

"Yeah, it's a nice little place." He smiled at me and then spotted mamma who had just come back in from the pantry.

"Good Afternoon Ma'am." He greeted her with a bow and took her hand to press a kiss on the top of it. She blushed and wiped her hands on her apron in nervousness.

"You must Edward…" she said with a little wink in my direction.

"Thank you for allowing me to join you today, I didn't mean to impose."

Mamma waved her hand around to dismiss what he'd just said. "You're not imposing; it'll be nice to have another pair of hands to help today."

I walked over to the stove and turned on the oven in preparation for the chicken that mamma was still plucking.

"Would you like me to do that ma'am?" Edward asked quickly and rolled his sleeves up. Mamma smiled and nodded, "If you wouldn't mind. It's not my most favourite task of the day."

Edward took over from mamma and quickly pulled the majority of the feathers from the body. I stepped back and made my way into the pantry, trying to find myself something that I could do whilst they were sorting out the meat; I hated watching it being prepared. I spotted a jar of mincemeat and remembered that mamma had said she didn't have any time to make some mince pies so I decided to start doing that, in the back corner of the kitchen.

***

Mamma was right; having an extra pair of hands was incredibly helpful in getting everything ready for dinner. We'd invited our neighbours and friends around for Christmas Eve dinner so nobody was left on their own on a night that could be potentially upsetting for everybody. Edward stood to leave as our guests started arriving.

"Where are you going?" Mamma asked quietly when he left the living room and bumped into her in the hallway.

"I was going to leave you to entertain your guests ma'am." He smiled and bowed again. "Thank you for having me over, it has been a lovely day."

Mamma patted her hands against her apron to brush off the stray bits of flour that were still covering her. "What are you doing tonight?"

"I'll probably grab a pie from the pub and then sit in my room for the evening."

Mamma shook her head vigorously and waved him away from the door. "Don't be daft, spend the evening here! I wouldn't want you all on your own."

Edward looked at the floor and rubbed the back of his neck with his hand. "I couldn't do that ma'am, I'd feel terrible for being in the way."

"Nonsense, I'll take more offence if you don't stay."

Edward looked up at me for help; I just shrugged and turned away with a small smirk. Mamma was sneaky but I wasn't going to complain if it meant I got to spend some more time with him.

"Oh, and please call me Beth. Ma'am was my mother."

***

Throughout the meal Edward was centre of attention and was kept busy by everybody asking him loads of questions, though he did find time to throw me a smile whenever there was a small lull in the conversation. Joan was sat on my right staring at me with pure envy.

"I regret taking you to the dance last night." She hissed as she leant across the table to reach the gravy, I tried to gauge whether she was joking or not because she sounded deadly serious. "If you hadn't have been there, he'd be with me right now."

I sighed and took a bite of the 'Canadian mash' that Edward had made for us. "He's not 'with me'. We're just getting to know each other."

Joan sighed and looked at me with a shake of her head. "Are you really that blind?"

I frowned and stared at the table in front of me. "Sorry?"

"He's very taken by you Rose! He hasn't taken his eyes off of you once tonight."

I blushed and glanced across at Edward to prove that he wasn't looking at me; instead I caught his eye and blushed a little more. He grinned at me before turning back to the conversation he was in.

"See! He clearly really likes you! And he seems like a right gentleman!"

I smiled and nodded, "he is."

"Exactly, and I was left with the rest of the soldiers and let me tell you, there isn't much that is gentlemanly about them."

"Guess I just got lucky then." I whispered through a happy sigh. Joan scowled.

"He spoke to me first!" she grumbled, I shook my head and laughed lightly.

"Clearly he likes me better." I raised an eyebrow as she turned red with anger and then stuck my tongue out. It was way too much fun winding up my friend.

***

Edward and I didn't get to talk much until the end of the night. I'd wandered into the back garden to get a breath of fresh air and was looking up at the stars when he crept up behind me and whispered 'boo' in my ear. I suppressed a scream and clamped my hand against my chest.

"Bloody hell!" I hissed as I whirled around to face him. "What are you trying to do? Kill me?"

He laughed and shook his head, "No, that's the last thing on my list."

I rolled my eyes and turned back to face the garden, looking up at the stars again.

"What are you doing out here?" He asked quietly.

"Watching the stars." I glanced back at him and gave him a small smile. "I do it when I'm missing people; it makes me feel connected to them in some way."

"How so?"

"Because I know that when they look up at the stars they see the same thing I do and it makes them seem slightly closer."

Edward smiled and perched on the garden wall. He patted the space next to him. "I found out when I'm due to leave England..." He whispered and crossed his arms over his chest.

"When...?" I asked slowly, I was a little unsure that I wanted to hear what he was about to say.

"In the next few days..." he muttered and glanced down at his hands. "I've been posted to France."

"Oh..."

He looked up at me and gave me a small smile. "I'm sorry; I wish I could stay longer."

I looked up to the sky and blinked away the tears that were forming. I didn't quite understand how I was getting so upset since I'd known him for merely a day, but I surely wasn't going to show him.

"It's all right, that's what you're here for isn't it? You're here to fight for your people." I spoke through a forced smile and blinked a few more times to try and rid myself of the tears.

He nodded slowly, "I just want to make the world a safe place again, so I can bring up a family without a worry." He turned to face me and took my hands in his.

"These past 24 hours have been some of the greatest of my life..."

I ducked my head in embarrassment, they had certainly been lovely but I didn't realise I was having such an effect on Edward. I felt his hand on my cheek as he moved my face until I was

36

looking him directly in the eye. Before I had a chance to say anything to him, he pressed his lips against mine. I gasped and pulled away hastily, I wasn't going to tell him that I wasn't comfortable with the kiss but I did need to stop him. The look that made itself evident on Edward's face was heart-breaking, he looked incredibly sad.

"I'm so sorry! I didn't mean to just pounce on you. Please forgive me."

I lifted a shaking hand to my lips and stared at him in shock.

"I'm just, I'm so scared of this war and I...I can't explain my actions. I'm sorry."

He stood up and quickly turned his back on me. I continued to stare at him, straining to hear what he was saying.

"I hadn't planned on that, I've been stopping myself the entire time we've been together. I just, I got overcome with emotion." He turned around to face me but kept his eyes focused on the button of his sleeve that he was toying with.

"I'm scared that I'm going to die and I didn't want to die without having kissed you." He glanced up at me briefly before returning his attention back to his button.

"You see, I really do think you're beautiful and you're the most wonderful gal I've ever spoken to and I'm just. I'm sorry."

I stood up and put another shaking hand against his shoulder.

"Don't worry." I mumbled, though he didn't hear me as he carried on apologising. I stood in front of him and gripped onto both of his arms this time, hoping he'd stop talking for long enough so I could tell him that it was all right.

"Edward, stop apologising. Admittedly, I was a little taken aback but it's fine. I understand."

He sighed and raised one hand to my face and caressed my cheek, I smiled and leant into it.

"I'm not usually this forward. I've been told I'm quite a gentleman."

I laughed and stroked both of his arms, "You are a gentleman." I squeezed lightly and gave him a small hug.

"A gentleman wouldn't have stolen a kiss off a lady like that." He mumbled sadly and dropped his hand. "A gentleman would have asked to have that kiss."

I watched him as he got increasingly upset with himself. "I'm not a true gentleman and I'm more than completely sorry."

He looked at me with watery eyes and smiled sadly; I shook my head and moved my hands from his arms to his face. I clasped his neck and made sure he was watching me.

"You are a gentleman. You're so very lovely and you've done nothing wrong."

"I should have asked you!"

"Then ask me."

Edward looked at me with wide eyes. "Sorry?"

"Ask me." I repeated and smiled at him. I knew I wasn't supposed to be encouraging him and in a perfect world I'd be supervised by my father whilst I was outside but since war had taken that opportunity away, I took my own opportunity from it.

"May I kiss you Rose?" Edward asked under his breath, a look of fear was evident as he waited for me to answer. I nodded slowly and stepped closer to him.

"Yes, you may."

He grinned before dipping his head; he cupped my cheek with his hand and pressed soft yet assertive kiss against my lips. He broke away quickly and grinned again as a blush spread across his nose.

"Was that better?" I asked sweetly and ran my fingers across his forearm before I reached his hand and linked our fingers.

"Yes. That's how it should have been the first time." He pressed another short kiss to my forehead and sighed.

****

Chapter Five

At first we stayed outside happily chatting but it was beginning to get incredibly cold, so we made our way back inside hurriedly. Mamma watched us walk in with a knowing smile on her face. I ducked my head as I blushed and quickly made my way over to the stove to start making cups of tea for everyone in an attempt to avoid that was imminent with mamma.

"Edward, what are you doing tomorrow?" she asked slowly when she'd stopped grinning at me. He pulled his coat off and walked into the room further.

"I'll be spending the day getting my paperwork ready for when I leave."

"Oh! When are you leaving?" She sat on one of the chairs around the kitchen table and motioned for Edward to join her.

"On the 27th ma'am," he glanced at me and smiled sadly, "which they only told me today."

I kept my attention split between the stove and the conversation at the table in case Edward was going to say something that I needed to hear.

"How long do you think that will take you?" Mamma questioned as she pulled the edge of table cloth taut. I hid a smile when I realised what she was going to ask.

"I'm not entirely sure, why do you ask?"

"Would you care to join us at dinner tomorrow?"

Edward looked slightly shocked by the question and sat stunned for a few seconds. "I'd love to, but I don't know if I'll have the time…"

Mamma's face fell, "the paperwork can wait, can't it? I mean you don't leave until the 27th! It would be lovely if you could join us for the festivities."

I quickly placed two cups of tea on the table from them and then left the room to hand out the rest of them. When I wandered back in, they were still arguing about it.

"I'd feel bad intruding! Christmas is a time to spend with family and I'm not really…family…" He threw me a small smile before looking back at mamma.

"Yes, but you see, I don't have half of my family around me anymore! There's plenty of space and plenty of food!" She shook her head slowly, "I don't want to be alone on Christmas…"

With a sigh of defeat, Edward nodded. "I'll see what I can do." Mamma jumped up from the table and patted his hand.

"Good. Good." She trotted out of the room with a smile. I quickly took the seat she vacated.

"I'm sorry about her Edward; she just misses having a man around the house."

"I wish you'd told me!"

I laughed, "How was I supposed to get that in the conversation? Anyway, she knows how to get what she wants."

Edward leant across the table and gathered my hands in his. "She won't be too upset if I don't manage to make it over, will she?"

I shook my head and gave his hands a squeeze. "Probably not, she'll be busy with the neighbours and entertaining the rest of guests. I'll make up some excuse if you'd prefer?"

Edward shook his head, "No, I'd rather not lie to her. Just remind her that I might be too busy to come over."

***

Mamma came back into the kitchen a little while later and moved us into the sitting room where the rest of the guests were stood around in a circle. The piano which was usually sat in the corner of the room, untouched throughout my childhood, was positioned in the centre of the circle; mamma quickly sat at it and tested the keys before starting to play Christmas hymns that we all knew. Edward wound his arm around my waist and pulled me into his side, giving me a small smile before he turned his attention to mamma and the song she was playing. It was a beautiful moment.

***

The time for Edward to leave came along way too soon. I wasn't ready to let him leave even though we'd spent the past hour or so, on our own, talking about our lives. My brothers had gone to bed and the other guests had already made their way home when mamma disappeared upstairs for a little while to give us time to chat.

"Will you come tomorrow?" I asked sadly whilst I grabbed my coat and ushered him outside. I clicked the door shut behind us and made sure that no light was visible.

"I don't know... I don't want to get in the way..."

I sighed and nodded, "Right, but the offer is still there okay?"

He smiled at me and we both stood in silence, watching each other as we thought of something else to say. Edward broke the silence first by quickly slapping both of his thighs and rummaging around his pockets. He grinned when he found a piece of folded paper and handed it to me.

"I thought that maybe, perhaps you could write to me when I'm away…" He looked a little sheepish and started to play with the button on his sleeve once again. I took the paper from him and smiled.

"That's very thoughtful of you, thank you." I turned to the front door. "Stay there!" I told him as I ran into the house and found some writing paper. I returned a few minutes later with my address written out. I handed it over to him and watched a smile spread across his face.

"In case you want to write me back." I bit my lip to stop from grinning and rocked onto the balls of my feet in excitement.

"I would be honoured." He neatly folded the piece of paper and slipped it into a pocket on the inside of his shirt. Edward glanced around and then sighed.

"Well, I best go. I don't want to walk into too many people on the way home." He laughed a little and clasped my hand. "Thank you for a lovely day." He brought my hand up to his mouth and pressed a kiss to the top of it. "Will you tell your mother that I say good night and Merry Christmas?"

I nodded and stepped down onto the step he was standing on, so we were level. "I will do. Have a safe journey back."

He stroked my hair. "I'll come by before I leave, okay?"

I gave him a sad smile and nodded my head before slowly wrapping my arms around his waist. "I hope you manage it, it would be awful for you to leave without saying goodbye."

"I'll never say goodbye to you, only see you soon." He smiled and hugged me tightly. "Plus, it gives me a reason to come back and see your brothers again!"

I laughed and stepped away from him. "They fell in love with you today." I mused and wrapped my arms around my middle to try and keep myself a little warmer.

"And I fell in love with them." He grinned and glanced at his watch. "Goodness, you must be freezing! Go back inside my darling and I will see you in a few days."

I nodded and walked back to the top step, I heard him clear his throat as my back was turned and I reached out to open the door. "Can I kiss you goodnight?" He muttered as a shaking hand reached out to touch my arm and draw me back to him. I nodded happily with a blush.

"Yes, of course."

He used one arm to pull me into him whilst using his other to cup my cheek before he pressed a very soft and very sweet kiss to the side of my mouth.

"Goodnight Rose." Edward gave me a small wave before he trotted down the garden and out of the gate. He waved once more and then turned to focus on where he was going. I sighed happily and leant against the door watching the night envelope his retreating form. My heart was hammering in my chest and my cheeks were still stained red by the blush that had spread across my face. I noticed that there were thousands of butterflies in my stomach and grinned when I realised how he made me feel. Edward McGraw was a true gentleman and I was falling for him, rather fast it appeared.

***

Sadly, Edward didn't manage to make it over for long on Christmas Day. He stopped by to tell mamma that they were going to be training for the rest of the day and then made a swift departure. In fact, the next time I saw him wasn't until he came by to say goodbye before he left. Before I got the chance to say anything to him, mamma had grabbed his arm and dragged him inside.

"When do you leave?" she asked as she forced him to sit at the table in the kitchen. My brothers' noticed he'd arrived and both came flying into the room with big smile on their faces.

"'ward!" Michael cried and threw his arms up in the air to get picked up. David happily sat by Edward's feet and carried on playing with his toy. Michael snuggled into his neck and sighed happily when he was put on Edward's knee.

"In 4 hours…" He finally answered mamma who was watching the scene in front of her with watery eyes and a sad smile.

"I'm glad you could make it around beforehand then." She poured him a cup of tea and sat next to him, asking him to fill her in on all the things he'd done over the past two days. I was left standing by the doorway of the kitchen, watching everything in annoyed amusement. It was annoying that he'd been taken away from me but it was amusing to watch my family fawn over somebody that wasn't my father.

During their conversation Edward kept looking over at me and after about the tenth time, mamma finally picked up on it. She looked between us two and then looked down sheepishly.

"Forgive me! I'll take the boys and leave you to it…" she smiled at me and tried to pry Michael away from Edward's arms, which was a feat much easier said than done. A ten minute fight ensued and finished with a lot of screaming and crying coming from both of the boys. Once they'd finally left us alone, I walked over to the table and sat down.

"I'm so sorry about that…" Edward apologised and leant across the table to kiss my cheek. I laughed and shook my head.

"Don't be silly, they're my family, I should be the one apologising."

Edward smiled and leant on his hands. "How are you?" he asked softly.

"I'm wonderful, thank you. How are you?" I asked with a small grin.

"Sad." He answered bluntly and looked over the top of my head as he focused on what he was trying to say. "I'm very sad. I don't want to leave."

"England isn't that amazing…" I retorted, "It probably holds nothing to Canada."

Edward snorted and shook his head, "It isn't because I'm in England that makes me not want to leave Rose…"

I clasped my hands together, laid them on the table and cocked my head to the side.

"Is it not?"

"It's because of you Rose." He looked at me pointedly. "I don't understand why I feel like this, but there is something about you that makes me never want to leave."

"There is?" I asked with a blush. I bit the side of my lip in nervousness and dropped my graze down to my hands.

"Yes! I never felt more connected to somebody than I have with you and we've only known each other for four days. Instead I feel like I've known you all my life."

He paused, "There's just something about you that is making me crazy and I really can't help how I'm feeling, even if it does seem to be a little…quick."

I wasn't sure what he wanted me to say so I kept my eyes trained on my hands and waited for him to carry on speaking.

"Rose, please say something…" he pleaded with me and gently touched my hands to get my attention. I flicked my gaze up to his and opened my mouth a few times before I shook my head and looked down again.

"I…I don't know what to say…"

46

He stood up abruptly and threw his hands in the air. "I feel like I've just opened up so much to you and it wasn't what you wanted to hear…" He walked over to the kitchen window and looked out over the garden. "I told you the other night that I'm scared. The way I feel about you is scary too." He turned back to face me and held his hands out in front of him in a sort of surrendering motion.

"I don't know what to do. I don't want to lose you but I don't feel it's fair to ask anything of you since I'm leaving…"

I watched him with my heart racing. "What do you want to ask?"

He rounded the table and knelt down next to me, turned me in my chair so I was facing him and took my hands in his. "I want to ask you to be mine. I want to ask you to love me. I want to ask you to marry me. I want to ask you to spend the rest of your life with me. I want to ask you everything!"

My heart leapt into my throat. "But you won't?" I questioned slowly, biting my lip to hide the grin that was threatening to spread across my face.

"I won't ask you that because I leave in less than 3 hours…"

I sighed and brought a hand up to stroke his face, "What if I wanted you to ask me that?"

"I would feel terrible because I can't make anything special for you, I can't do anything special for you…"

I shook my head and raised my other hand to his face so I was holding it steady. "I don't care. I don't care that you're being taken away; I don't care that you might not come back. I want you to ask me."

"Rose, I can't!" He pressed a kiss into the palms of my hands. "I want to, but I can't."

I sat back in my chair with an exhausted sigh. "Don't you mean you won't…?"

"Rosie, don't be like that. I would give you the world if I could."

"Then ask me!"

"Rosie..."

I stood up and walked over to the sink to give myself something to do. I left Edward kneeling on the floor and when I turned to face him, I found that he was still in exactly the same position. "I feel the same..."

I played with my nails and expression, "I feel the same, which is why I want you to ask me..."

He stood up and moved to my side as fast as he could. "You mean, if I were to ask, the answer would be yes?"

I nodded and bit my lip again to suppress the grin. Edward's face lit up for a split second before it clouded again. "I can't...it isn't fair."

"What isn't fair is denying this, denying us something when you're leaving me!" I snapped and blushed at my outburst. "It doesn't matter if you ask me or not, you've already got my heart. It's just a matter of you realising it."

Edward looked at me shocked, "I...I do?"

I nodded and wiped my hands on the sides of my dress in nervousness. "You had me at hello..."

***

Mamma ended up coming back into the kitchen a few minutes after I'd told him how I felt and sat with us as we shared a cup of tea. She kept watching me with a look of contemplation on her face and I wondered if she'd heard any of our conversation, though that thought didn't stay in the forefront of my mind however, because Edward had just glanced up at the clock and noticed the time.

"Well I guess that I should get going. I don't want to be late."

Mamma and I stood at the same time to say goodbye, she threw her arms around his neck and squeezed him tightly. "Stay safe Edward, I expect to see you here in one piece when the war is over."

I smiled sadly and linked my hands with his as we walked to the front door. "I'll be back soon okay?" he mumbled and kissed the back of my hand.

"When will you write me?" I asked slowly, it was a silly question but I didn't know how long I'd have to wait without hearing from him.

"Oh! That reminds me!" He started patting down his legs again before he found what he was looking for and handed me a small envelope with an elegantly scrawled 'Rose' across the front. "Don't open it until you really miss me."

I nodded and clutched the envelope in my hand. Edward stepped forward and kissed my cheek before he turned to leave.

"See you soon my darling!" he called before I caught his hand and pulled him towards me so I could hold him tightly. He pressed another kiss to the side of mouth and then waved goodbye. "Keep watching those stars, I'll always be looking back."

****

Chapter Six
1940

Rosie,

I hope that you waited until you really missed me to read this letter. I am sorry that I had to leave so abruptly. I am also very sorry that I couldn't make anything more special for you – I know that this is important. I have wanted to be a soldier ever since I was a little boy but for once I wish I had not made that decision. I wish I had not signed up as quickly as I did, then I could have given you a normal life instead of expecting you to wait around for me. Although, I would not have come to England if it was not for the war, so I suppose there is a better side to it, if you think of it in that way. I don't have much more to say because everything I have needed or wanted to say, I have already told you. Just know that I will make you mine, officially, when this war is over. It would please me to no end if you became Mrs. Rose McGraw. I will see you soon my love.

Edward.

***

The beginning of 1940 was quite inconsequential. Nothing major happened bar the fact we were thrown head first into a war that we knew nothing about or had any experiences in. In fact, the only real reminder that anything was happening left with the Canadian soldiers, who were shipped out in two different waves.

Edward left on the 27th December with his wave and the rest left after the New Year.

A lot of people assumed that Prime Minister Neville Chamberlain had gotten things wrong and that the war had ended almost as quickly as it started and that he hadn't thought to tell the British public. Other people got a little upset about what was being said about the Prime Minister and fought his corner quite forcefully. All I knew was that we were calling the period 'The Phony War' and that name stuck.

***

To keep my mind off of the misery that had threatened to engulf me since Edward left, I kept myself busy by splitting my time between the kitchen and library. I baked, I cooked, I sewed and I read, but nothing was detracting from the monotony that had enveloped my life. I felt bad for constantly complaining to mamma since she had so much to deal with, but she knew something was wrong and assured me that she wanted to know.

This meant that we spent many early mornings, awake before the sun, sat by the stove drinking cups of coffee and chatting. I would explain how I just wanted to do something with my life so I wouldn't go insane with boredom; she simply just stated that she wished she could bring my father back. This fact had her breaking down and crying more than I'd ever seen her cry before.

"Mamma, what are we going to do?" I asked from the warm nest of my folded arms one morning.

"About what?" Mamma questioned as she put a cup of coffee in front of me and nudged me to move.

"Our lives…" I watched her face for a few minutes, half expecting it to cloud over like it usually did. Instead, surprisingly, she gave me a bright smile.

"Well, I'm glad you asked actually!" She clapped her hands together gleefully. I raised an eyebrow in question.

"You are?"

She nodded, "Yes! You see, I was talking to Old Pam down by the butchers and she told me that they're looking for recruitments…"

"The butchers are looking for recruitments?"

Mamma frowned for a few seconds and then shook her head.

"No…the…thing? You know!"

I giggled, "Mamma, I can safely say that I have no idea what you're talking about…"

She sighed and leant her forehead against her hands in thought and frustration. I took a sip of my coffee and pulled a face at the fact it was lukewarm.

"Oh! I remember! The Home Guard is looking for female recruitments to take over some of the posts so they can free some men up for war."

"Oh…right…" I scrunched my nose up and pinched the bridge of it. "What do they want us to do?"

"Old Pam didn't tell me that much, she just mentioned that there was some form of recruitment meeting this week."

"When?"

"Tomorrow I believe, early afternoon, down at the school." I smiled gratefully and stood up to leave the room.

"Well, I should probably get dressed and write Edward back! Thank you for letting me know about everything mamma."

She nodded and smiled, "do you mind waking the boys up for me?"

I shook my head and walked upstairs, the daily cycle had started once again.

***

By the time I arrived at the school the following day, everywhere was packed full of people. I was a little surprised by the amount of people who wanted to sign up but joined the end of the queue nonetheless. I'd asked Joan to come with me since we hadn't seen each other since before Christmas but she'd declined and had explained that she 'had better things to do with her time'. So I was left standing in the school hall, on my own, completely mesmerised by the lengthy line of women.

"What are you here for?" A young girl, who looked to be just a bit older than me, asked with a smile.

"I was told the Home Guard is looking for recruitments…" I shrugged and smiled a little. The girl nodded her head and flicked her jet black hair over one shoulder.

"They are, you're correct, but they're recruiting for many things. Which one are you going for?"

"Oh! I didn't know there were options…I was just going to put my name down."

The girl laughed and stuck her hand out in front of me. "The names Betty, what's yours?"

"Rose." I took her hand and shook it. "What are you signing up for?" I asked her. She grinned at me and then dragged me over to her relevant line.

"I was signing up to work with the ambulances, as a driver or as dispatch, I don't mind."

I nodded and then looked around the room with a frown.

"What else is there to do?"

Betty shrugged, "I think there are wardens and lookouts, none of them seem that interesting."

"Right…"I hesitated and wondered what I wanted to do.

"You should sign up with me! That way I'd have the opportunity to be with somebody I knew!"

I laughed and shook my head slowly, "Well…"

"I know I don't know you properly, but by the time anything happens we'll probably be old friends."

I sighed and watched as the queue moved faster than any others in the room. "Fine, I'll sign up. Though if we're not together, I won't be happy…"

Betty clapped her hands together, "Oh how exciting! I was scared about signing up on my own."

With a laugh I stepped towards the table, "I thought as much"

A very bored looking lady glanced up at me with a judging expression. "Name?" she barked.

"Rose Andrews." I replied shyly.

"Age?"

"18." She stopped what she was doing and scrutinised me.

"18 you say?" Her lips were pursed together tightly and she raised an eyebrow.

I nodded. I wasn't sure why she was questioning me and it was making me a little nervous.

"Right, Date of Birth." She continued barking at me.

"May 14th 1921."

"Address."

I gave over where I lived and was very quickly ushered away by a sharp "Next!"

Betty wandered over a few minutes later with a giggle. "Well, she was rude!"

"Why did she question me about being 18?"

Betty sighed and pulled me away from the school hall. "A lot of people have been lying about their ages to try and help. They needed to make sure."

"Do I look younger than 18?"

She snorted and shook her head, "Nah, you look like you're 40. Come on. Let's go, you only live down the street from me." Betty started nattering away about different things she'd heard about the war but I wasn't paying much attention to anything she was saying – I was still trying to figure out why I looked younger than 18.

"Have you been listening to anything I've said?" Betty snapped a little while later, I glanced over at her in panic.

"Yes..."

She rolled her eyes and then stopped walking. "I said, what made you sign up?"

"I was bored with my life since Edward left."

"Who is Edward?" she asked softly, "Is he a brother or something?"

I smiled brightly, "No. Edward is one of the Canadian soldiers. He's my...well...he's..."

"He's what?"

"I don't know. We never really made anything official. He just said he wanted to marry me when the war was over."

She clasped her hands to her chest and sighed. "Oh! How wonderfully romantic!"

I nodded happily and started to walk up the street again.

"When does he get back?"

I shrugged, "I don't know. I'm waiting on a letter from him as it is. It could be any time."

"Oh! Can we go to the post office? I want to see if you have a letter!"

I rolled my eyes but nodded all the same. "Okay, sure. I doubt I have though, he only sent one a few weeks ago."

***

As it turned out, I did actually have a letter waiting from Edward at the post office and mamma had a couple from my father and my brother. Much to Betty's dismay, I refused to open the letter in front of her, but promised that I'd let her read it the next time I bumped in to her. She assured me that it would be the following day if she had anything to do with it.

"Mamma!" I cried when I came home, I was more excited about her letters than I was mine. "Mamma, come here!" She came running out of the kitchen with a panicked look, it immediately disappeared when she realised that I was smiling.

"What? What's happened?"

I grinned at her and handed her the top envelopes, she wiped her hands on the side of her apron and took them from me slowly. "They're not…telegrams…are they?"

I shook my head still smiling, "Nope, they're letters…"

She squealed and ran into the living room before ripping them open. Within seconds she breathed a sigh of relief. "They're safe. They're both safe. So is my brother."

I nodded and wrapped my arms around her, "I'm glad. Thank goodness."

She gave me a watery smile and carried on reading her letters. I sat on the chair at the other side of the room and opened mine with shaking hands.

Rose,

I am sorry it has taken so long for me to write you back. It has been a little bit hectic with moving around and such. I am safe though, safe and missing you more than anything.

I hope you are well and I look forward to hearing from you with your new adventures, I would tell you what was going on but as you know, company policy.

See you soon my darling,

Edward.

***

I heard back from the Home Guard a few months later, it was 4 days before my 19th birthday. It was also the same day that my aunt came barging into the house, throwing her belongings everywhere. I heard her crashing about downstairs from my room at the back of the house and immediately felt sorry for mamma. I hovered at the top of the stairs and tried to figure out what was going on but all I could hear was muffled voices as they wandered around the kitchen. I darted out of sight when Victoria came slamming out of the kitchen, wailing about how she couldn't cope without her husband and how ridiculous the news broadcast she'd been listening to was.

"Bleeding Chamberlain got it wrong didn't he? That's why he's stepping down as Prime Minister." I had wandered downstairs and was about to head into the kitchen when I heard Victoria shouting in the living room. I peered around the door and glanced at the two women sat in there. Mamma had her head buried in her hands and was shaking whereas Victoria was marching around the room with a face like thunder.

"He gets our men to go out there and fight and there's bloody nothing happening! So what does he do? Run away! The bleeding cheek of it!"

I walked into the room slowly and cleared my throat. Mamma glanced up and looked relieved to see me. She mouthed a quick thank you and then continued to bury her head in her hands.

"What's going on?" I asked. My aunt whirled on me and narrowed her eyes.

"Listen to the wireless. Listen to what they're telling us now! I don't bloody believe it."

I walked nearer to the radio so I'd be able to hear it over the noise of my aunt and waited until the news story continued.

"I am speaking to you from 10 Downing Street, where we have just been informed that Neville Chamberlain is resigning as Prime Minister and Winston Churchill will be stepping up. No details of the reasoning have been released yet but we will inform you when there is any new information."

Victoria huffed and dropped to the chair in annoyance. "He takes my man away," she paused before looking at both mamma and me. "...*Our* men away, for a war that isn't happening and now...now he's resigning!" she shook her head in despair. "I knew he was useless."

I turned the radio off before anything more could be said to annoy her even further.

"You don't know what is happening out there..." I mentioned quietly with a quick glance to the door. I didn't want the boys hearing any of this. "You don't know what is happening just over the water. None of us do."

Victoria narrowed her eyes yet again, "Nothing is happening! That's my bloody point. Why would he resign if there is actually a war that he started? It's embarrassment! He's ashamed of himself."

I rolled my eyes and quickly put an arm around mamma, since she was beginning to shake again.

"I get letters from Edward, he says that things are worse than they imagined.

Victoria snorted and then stood up again, she stormed over to me a started to, quite viciously, poke me in the shoulder.

"Your boyfriend can't tell you anything. Careless talk costs lives apparently, so why would he tell you what it's like?"

"I didn't say he said anything about what it was like, he just said it was worse than they imagined."

"If they imagined nothing was happening and there's a tiny fight, then that's worse isn't it? You can't prove anything."

I was seconds away from retorting when mamma shot out of her chair, grabbed her sister's arm and took her to the front door.

"Firstly," she hissed through gritted teeth. "Never poke my daughter like that." She grabbed Victoria's coat and thrust it out to her.

"Secondly, there's a perfectly reasonable explanation for what's going on so you needn't be so rude about a man that has tried to do his best for us!" Mamma opened the door so forcefully that I was surprised it didn't get ripped off its hinges.

"Thirdly, Chamberlain didn't take our men. Our men went willingly, that's a massive difference." She pushed her sister to the top of the stairs out of the door.

"Finally, get out! And don't you dare bother coming back until you're much calmer. I can't deal with you anymore."

In a flurry of anger, she slammed the door in Victoria's face and all but screamed at the back of it.

**

"I'm sorry about that Rose…" Mamma apologised a little while later when she'd calmed down enough to stop getting angry at everything. "I shouldn't have let her talk to you like that."

I shrugged and smiled. "It doesn't matter, don't worry. The war has gotten everybody het up – it's fine."

Mamma slammed her hands on the kitchen table and groaned. "I don't understand why the fact that her husband has left is much worse for her than it is for me." She shook her head in confusion. "I don't understand why this war is affecting her far more than it is anybody else."

I patted her hands gently and tried to calm her down. "That's just what she's like mamma. She always has been – you know that. Everything is always so much worse for her."

"She infuriates me, I probably shouldn't have thrown her out but I've seriously had enough."

"Mamma, she had it coming." I smiled sadly, "Don't worry about it, you've done nothing wrong."

She didn't seem to accept that what she had done was understandable, so I tried to think of something to tell her that would take her mind off of what had just transpired.

"Oh! Mamma, do you remember when I went to the school to join the Home Guard?" I didn't wait for an answer; instead I just carried on talking.

"Well I met this girl, Betty Foster and she convinced me to sign up to work with the ambulances.

Mamma nodded and gave me a small smile.

"I got a letter this morning; they want me to start training in the next couple of months!"

****

Chapter Seven

Training for the Home Guard started in early June and spanned the rest of the summer. I didn't think it was going to be as difficult as it actually was, I thought it would be a few talks about what to do and where to go in different situations, but I had assumed entirely wrong. Although it was hard work, I soon realised just how nice it was to be able to get out of the house for a while.

The threat of civilian bombings was ever increasing, especially as the Germans had started attacking the docklands and the ports all over the country, so the first thing they trained us in was safe evacuations. At least three times a week we had an evacuation practice, whether it was at a bustling dock, a busy warehouse or a lone house in the middle of the street, we were expected to handle each situation with responsibility and logic whilst assuring everybody that they were going to be safe.

This meant that we were expected to stand our ground when somebody decided they didn't want to follow our orders and had a check list to go through when everybody was out of the building. On top of that, we then had to swiftly move everybody to safety which would either be a basement in a nearby building or the nearest air raid shelter.

There was one evacuation where I had to deal with one of the most arrogant and irritating people during a practice at a munitions factory. He stood in front of me and very sternly told me that he wasn't going to move without good reason. No matter how many times I explained to him that it was a practice and he needed to move – otherwise it'd make things difficult for other people – he wouldn't listen.

"Tell me why I should listen to you young lady!" He spat and continued to stand in the middle of the building whilst others listened to their representative and left, albeit against their will but they left.

"I'm sorry Sir, but you need to vacate the building otherwise you're putting your life and others' at risk."

"I'm not though, am I?"

"Excuse me Sir, please ask questions when we're a safe distance away from the building."

"You can't swan in here with your clipboard and fancy uniform and expect me to listen to a thing that you have to say!"

"Pardon me Sir, but there is no need to be so disruptive. We're doing this for your safety. If this was a real alarm then you'd be in serious danger."

He slapped his hands against his thighs and looked at me with wary eyes. "I don't have to listen to a word you say young lady! I'm much older than you, therefore I know more than you and I'm pretty sure that there isn't a problem right now."

He turned his back to me and continued with his work. I sighed and looked around me for help, Betty sent me a sympathetic smile and shrugged one shoulder as she ushered peopled out of the factory. I quickly mouthed to her 'get Tommy' and then turned my attention back to the petulant man in front of me.

"Excuse me Sir; you can carry on your work when the practice is over, until then will you please step outside?"

He ignored me and moved further down the conveyer belt to continue with his next step. I felt Tommy, a senior officer, tap me on the arm; he cocked his head towards the door and told me to leave. I walked out just as I heard raised voices coming from behind me.

"Unless you want me to report you for obstructing a practice raid that is being carried out under the government's orders, I suggest you get yourself outside rather swiftly!"

I smiled as the door shut behind me.

***

The public were still experiencing air raid practices most days, which was where our training took us next. They made sure that we were able to direct people quickly and efficiently to their nearest shelter and they made sure that we were capable of dealing with extremely terrified members of the public without causing the panic to spread across to others. We were also told to make sure that everybody was carrying their gas masks at all times, in case Hitler started to attack us with poisonous gasses. At first we had all been given maps to jot down where the specific air raid shelters were and what the safest and quickest route to them was, but after about two weeks of training, we were expected to have remembered everything off by heart. It wasn't that difficult if you were going to be stationed at a specific part in London, but if you were one of the unlucky ones that had to work all over the capital, then trying to remember everything was agonisingly tough.

There were more than 10 shelters per area, each were named by their specific street and what building or house they were next to or near to. Thankfully, we were give clipboards to jot down ones that we couldn't remember properly but it didn't help when everybody was in a rush to find the closest one.

The closest one also depended on what part of a street you were stood on and if you were found sending people to a shelter that was marginally further away, then you'd get a stern talking to and the proverbial slap on the wrists. It was during this part of my training that I wondered if perhaps I'd signed up for the wrong thing. It was tiresome, difficult and not at all fun, but I powered through and was looking forward to the next part of our training.

Following this, we were then split into various sections of the Home Guard and trained on our posts. My section was the last to be decided and I was worried, for a short while, that we were going to be given something entirely different to what we'd initially put our names down for. Thankfully Betty was with me and we both stood there, nervously yet patiently waiting to find out what was going on. Betty and I were lead to an underground office system that was full of phones and maps with drawing pins dotted over them. Above one of the main maps on the centre of the main wall, the words 'Ambulance Dispatch' had been written. I felt Betty relax next to me as I sighed in relief, we were going to be working in the centre of the Home Guard, the heart that would help keep everything running and just looking at the room was filling me with a sort of excitement. That was until the lady that had been barking at me when I signed up walked into the room with a stern expression on her face.

"Welcome to Ambulance Dispatch. The safety of the public is now in your hands."

She eyed us all and handed out the standard issue uniforms.

"These must be worn at all times." She pointed to the hates, "and your hair must be pulled off of your face. You need to look smart all the time." She stared at us. "You must all refer to me as Ma'am. I am nothing else."

Within minutes of her walking into the room, she had us all sat around the table and was barking out rules and regulations that we had to follow before ushering us out of her sights so we could get changed into the proper attire.

"Well, this sounds like it's going to be fun…" Betty whispered sarcastically as the woman walked back into the room. I suppressed a snort and nodded slightly.

"Several of you will work in here, the centre of the dispatch, whereas others of you will be working alongside the ambulance drivers, making sure that they get to their destination in the quickest time possible."

We were stood in a line and Ma'am, with her hands clasped firmly behind her back, walked up and down staring at us all in disdain.

"You are the only people responsible for the speed of the ambulances. You'll know where the bombs have hit and what roads are inaccessible and it's down to you to pass these messages on as quickly and as efficiently as possible."

I rocked onto the balls of my feet in excitement, as scary as the responsibility sounded, I was looking forward to being able to get started.

"The training for this will begin at the end of August, but be prepared. You need to know London like the back of your hand and if you don't already, then I suggest that you hurry up and learn it."

***

The threat of war was starting to become very real as news of what was happening in France began to hit England. The Dunkirk landings ended with thousands upon thousands of men stranded in occupied France and it took boats of all sizes, including fishing boats, to get all the men back to England. Churchill tried to play it off as the best thing that could've happened since we all pulled together to work as a community, but we all knew differently. From there, the Battle of Britain was soon in full swing with German bombers flying over the docklands and bombing them to try and keep our boats away from their advancing soldiers. None of it worked though and we stood united as a country, determined to keep the evil out.

The day we found out about the fall of France was one of the scariest moments I'd had up until then. Betty had come over to deliver the newest addition of our uniform, a badge that let senior officers know what section we were working in, when she told me the news.

"France has fallen to The Nazi's. They're advancing to England next." She hissed when she'd dragged me into the cupboard under the stairs to make sure we weren't overheard.

"No…!"

She nodded, though I could barely see this in the dark space.

"Yes, it has. We need to be prepared."

I nodded and then gasped as I remembered that Edward was over in France, at least, that's where he'd initially said he was being stationed.

"Edward?" Betty asked softly, I nodded.

"I don't know if he's safe. I mean, wouldn't he have back here if he was stranded? What if he's injured?" I started panicking and shuffled around until I was by the door and could open it to let some light and fresh air in.

"He's fine, you'll see. Don't worry. He's probably finding it difficult to write to you to let you know that he's okay."

"I hope so…" I mumbled sadly. "I'm scared."

Betty wandered out of the closet and hugged me to her, "I know you are darling, but everything is going to be okay, you'll see."

***

Although France had fallen and the bombings on the docks were becoming much worse, England didn't really see such much more action. However that changed on the day of September 7th

– what started off as a quiet bombing reached levels unexpected by almost every citizen in Britain.

It was around 3pm when the first bomb hit the streets of London, thankfully I wasn't near this one, but news travelled fast and people wanted to see the destruction it caused. I remember seeing the burning inferno of the house that had been hit and hoping that the people who had been living there weren't home at the time. A little while later another bomb was dropped on London, and then another, and then another – the Blitz had started and we weren't aware what this would mean for all of us. Ambulance dispatch was called, but I wasn't required to attend, instead they left it to the senior officers and I was told to keep my street safe.

***

Initially we thought that this campaign of Hitler's would pass quickly, but we were incredibly mistaken. A few nights later I was awoken by the air raid siren wailing. I knew that this was definitely a time to get into the air raid shelter instead of lying in a warm bed.

"Rose! Get up! Help me with the boys!" My mother shouted for me through the house. I grabbed my shoes and a coat I'd left upstairs just in case and followed my mother into my brothers' room.

"Wake them up!" She hissed as she made her way to David. I rushed over to Michael and tried my hardest to wake him up as quickly as possible. When his bleary eyes opened and looked up at me, I bundled him in his bed sheet and carried him downstairs as fast as I could, mamma was hot on my heels.

"Anderson Shelter! Now. Quickly!" She shouted above the loud air raid siren. There was a loud grumbling bang from somewhere down the street and the world was illuminated for a couple of seconds before everything fell black again.

"Run Rose! Get into the shelter now!" Mamma screamed and ran up behind me. "That one was so close, we could be next!"

I suddenly wished that my father was here to calm her down because she was causing me to panic which was upsetting both of the boys and was making the journey down the garden much harder than necessary. Once we'd flung the door open, set the boys on the bunks and closed the door again, she'd managed to stop shouting instead she was shaking extremely badly.

"I thought that was it for a minute." She mumbled in sadness and sat down next to David with her arms wrapped around her middle. I winced as I heard another bomb explode from around our street and perched on the bunk opposite her.

"We're fine; we're safe in here now." I gave her a reassuring smile and took a deep breath to steady my nerves. I didn't believe it as such but I knew I had to keep my mother calm for the boys' sake; inside I was a panicking mess and was completely certain we weren't going to make it out alive. I guess this was what Edward meant when he said 'you don't know what's going on'.

With lack of something to do, I sat and listened as the planes groaned over us before depositing their heavy loads onto the unsuspecting houses below. I hoped Joan was all right because she'd left her aunts and had returned to the nurses' station. At least, I thought bitterly, she'd not feel helpless now.

"The boys are asleep," Mamma told me in wonderment, indeed they'd covered their heads, curled up and had fallen asleep again.

"I want to be able to sleep through it…" she whispered and buried her head in her hands. "I hope John and your father are okay" she muttered as an afterthought.

I sighed and listened out for the drone of planes again, it was eerily silent.

"Mamma, why don't you lie down and try and get some sleep? The siren will go off again when it's safe for us to leave."

Mamma nodded and laid down behind David, cuddling him into her. "What about you?" she mumbled as her eyes drifted shut.

"Don't worry; I'll keep an ear out for the siren. You need to look after the boys in the morning."

She nodded, gave me a smile and yawned before she quietened.

I felt awful for the families that would've been affected by the bombing, but since we were caught so unaware by the planes, I couldn't get ready safely and get to work. I knew I was going to suffer some flak from Betty and Ma'am but there was nothing I could do.

I sighed and leant my head back against the corrugated iron wall. It was silent outside, I couldn't hear planes, I couldn't hear screaming and the siren had stopped. Part of me hoped that anybody who got injured died instantly so they didn't have to suffer and another part of me hoped that everybody managed to get away safely, even though the likelihood of that was slim.

I felt my eyes start to drift shut and let myself relax for a few minutes, daydreaming that it was summer and I was in a field dancing happily with Edward. I managed to even convince myself that I could feel the sun on my face and the breeze against my skin – that was until I was abruptly brought back to reality by another wave of planes. As the first bomb dropped and exploded a distance away, I looked over my family, thankful that they managed to sleep through it.

****

Chapter Eight

Everyone thought that the bombings were going to peter out, especially when Hitler realised that he had started to hit the towns and cities instead of his original targets but it became apparent, after a week of near constant bombing that this wasn't going to be the case.

It was then that people started to worry about what the war was going to bring them. We'd already suffered through the Battle of Britain, which was entirely fought in the air, and were hearing horror stories from the men rescued from France but nobody was entirely prepared for the attack on the nation.

It soon became second nature to dive into an air raid shelter the second the alarm was sounded in case it wasn't a practice. I had heard many stories from friends about the crammed underground stations that people were sleeping in as the raids ended up happening during the night more than anything.

As one of the front runners of the Home Guard, I was expected to report the bombing sites and dispatch emergency services there as fast as I could, but at times I'd have to take on a role that meant being outside in the horrifying streets as buildings exploded around us. I'd been saved more times that I was happy to admit by passing guardsmen as they saw a building fall to its foundations near me. I never slept more than 3 or 4 hours a night and that was if I was lucky. The further we got into the year and the bombing spree, the more times I ended up spending days on end awake and surviving on coffee.

I knew that some of the horrific things I had seen would end up staying with me until the day I died, especially when it involved the remnants of bodies that had been badly injured in one of the many blasts that would occur over night.

The first time I'd ever seen a dead person was when I helped clean up and sort out a street in East London and I hadn't stopped screaming. I wasn't sure if it was more in despair that those people had lost their lives or in fear, but I didn't stop until Betty whacked me around the face and told me to get a grip. From then on, I tried to detach myself from everything. Instead of being a human being with feelings and fears, I became a shell of myself – I knew when it was the right time to be caring and sympathetic but I managed to no longer feel as affected by the horrific scenes as I once had.

***

I had the real shock of my life in November 1940, in the middle of another nightly bombing.

"Rose! You need to call Pat." Betty hissed as she flew into our little underground office. "You need to call him straight away, ambulances are needed immediately."

"Right, where am I sending them?" I grabbed the phone and dialled the numbers, waiting impatiently as I listened to the ringing. I glanced up at Betty; her face was a peculiar cross between sympathy and sadness.

"Swiss Cottage."

My entire body went cold with fear. "S...Swiss Cottage?"

She nodded her head slowly and clamped a hand on my shoulder.

"Hello? Hello? Rose is that you?"

I heard the voice calling in my ear and cleared my throat as I tried to focus on the job at hand.

"Pat, you need to get some ambulances down to Swiss Cottage."

"How many?"

I repeated the question to Betty, "How many?"

"As many as he can get there…" She winced. I closed my eyes, took in a breath and bit my lip. It must've been hit badly.

"As many as you can Pat, just get them there."

"Need me to pick you up?"

"Please."

I hung up the phone and grabbed my helmet, my gas mask and my coat.

"How bad is it?" I asked Betty as we scrambled into the street.

"You…just…" She took a deep breath and patted my shoulder again, "Rose, I'm sorry."

***

We stood on the side of the street, listening to the approaching wailing sirens and watching the scared people ducking for cover as they tried to help through the bombing. Pat pulled up against the curb as quick as he could and gave me a panicked look.

"IN!" He shouted and threw the ambulance into drive as I managed to get seated. I chanced one more look at Betty, who was waving us off with a sad smile, and knew I that wasn't going to be anywhere near prepared for what I was about to see.

"Have you seen it?" I asked slowly while Pat was maneuvering around people and the debris scattered all over the road. He nodded and glanced over at me, I noticed that his face was an ashen grey.

"Rosie, darling, I'm sorry."

72

I nodded and stared out of the window, trying to rid myself of any attachment I had to Swiss Cottage for the time I was going to be there helping, though I knew it hadn't worked when we got to the top end of the street. Pat didn't say anything to me; he jumped out of the ambulance and started to help the people nearest to him.

I didn't recognise where I was at first. The street was in complete ruins, there were fires burning everywhere I looked and families were stood holding each other in tears as that looked at the damage inflicted on their homes. People that I'd known my entire life were not either stood wailing on the street or were lying deadly silent among the rubble. I fled down the road to inspect the damage nearer mamma's house and immediately fell to my knees when I saw that it no longer existed. The house, which had once stood proud atop of stairs and a garden gate was just a front wall and half a kitchen. I looked around for my mother in panic. Pat and one of his nurses came over to me and each put an arm around me.

"Where are they?" I asked quickly and tried to pull away from them as they took me away from the front of the house.

"Where have they gone?" I cried and stood my ground, they called another male over to help move me.

"Are they safe?" I screamed this time, nobody was answering me and I needed to know what was going on.

"Rose, come with us." Pat hissed, he grabbed my arm and near on dragged me away. "You need to calm down; this isn't going to be easy."

Somebody gave him a cold cloth to press against my head but I wasn't paying attention, all I could concentrate on was the bodies on the ground that he'd stopped me near. There was one adult and two little children, all were covered by a white sheet. I looked up at Pat, my eyes already filling with tears that I wasn't ready to cry. He nodded quickly and pulled back the top of the sheet, slowing me a quick glimpse at their faces.

"Mamma!" I screamed and fell to my knees for a second time. I ripped the sheet away and looked at the faces of my two younger brothers before starting to sob. They all looked peaceful and I was glad that they weren't suffering the pain of their missing limbs, but it wasn't fair. Especially not for the boys, they'd not even reached their fifth birthday and their lives had been snatched away from them.

I ran a hand across their faces and continued to sob, screaming in protest as I was pulled away from them and taken to a different part of the street.

"Rose!" I watched as Pat started shouting something at me but I couldn't hear anything. His mouth was moving but there was no noise, in fact I couldn't hear anything that was being said by anyone – it was as if I'd suddenly gone deaf.

"Rose, look at me!"

Still I couldn't make out what he was saying. I looked around the street to see if anybody else was having the same problem and noticed that everything seemed to be moving in slow motion and high speed at the same time.

"Rose, you need to focus."

I turned my attention back to Pat and frowned before everything became black and I felt myself falling.

***

I opened my eyes slowly and squinted at the bright light being shone in them.

"Rose, are you okay?" A voice in the far distance asked me. "Did you hit your head when you fell?"

I closed my eyes and was quickly sucked under into nothingness again. The second time I opened my eyes, I was lying in a room I didn't recognise, surrounded by people who kept casting concerned glances over at me.

"Will she be okay?" Betty asked a man who had his back to me.

"She should be, it was just a lot for her to take in."

Betty groaned and pulled off her hat in despair. "I knew I should've gone with her…or instead of her."

The man turned around so I could see him, I realised that it was Pat and he was walking towards me. "She needed to know Betty, there's nothing you could've done differently."

"I could've been there!"

"I was there, it didn't help. She fainted and that's all that happened."

I snapped my eyes shut before they could notice I was awake. I had momentarily forgotten why I'd fainted by the instance I remembered, I didn't want to wake up.

"Rose, there's no point pretending you're not awake. I just saw your eyes open."

I peered out of one and up at Pat who was smiling softly, "You need to get up Rose otherwise we can't help those people out there." He jerked his head in the direction of the door and tried to sit me up.

"I don't want to." I snapped and lay back down. I was being petulant, I knew that but I didn't want to face the reality of my family's death.

"I know you don't, but you have to." He grumbled and grabbed my arm. I bit back a scream and looked helplessly at Betty.

"Pat, go easy on her, she's not herself." Betty removed Pat's hand from my arm and wound hers around my waist. "Come on, let's get you home."

I stumbled as my feet touched the ground and burst into tears.

"I don't have a home!"

Betty sighed and made sure I didn't fall over. "Yes you do, you're staying with me. You'll be safe there."

"But what about my things?" I mumbled brokenly. I'd brought a lot of my personal belongings with me in a bag since I'd spent most of the time in Central London, but I'd lost a lot in the house too.

"Anything you desperately need, can be replaced Rose."

She patted me on the back and got me out of the room so Pat could use the space.

"My letters from Edward?" I whispered. "What about my letters from Edward?"

"They're in your bag darling. Stop worrying, you just need to sleep. Let me get you back to mine." She bit her lip in annoyance as she tried, and failed, to get me outside.

"Where's my bag?" I didn't know where I was, but I still looked around the room frantically for my leather tote.

"It's already at my flat. Rose, for the love of God, come on!"

***

When she managed to get me back to her place, she laid me on the sofa and covered me with a blanket.

"I have to go back to work and hold down the base, will you be all right without me?"

I nodded slowly and snuggled into the blanket. I'd be all right; I was only planning on sleeping the day away. She stroked my hair gently and gave me a soft smile before leaving as quickly as she could. I closed my eyes and attempted to fall into a blissful sleep but that wasn't going to happen easily. Every time I shut my eyes I ended up seeing the faces of my family and the blood stained sheets that covered the horrific injuries they had sustained.

I was so used to being able to go home for Sunday dinner after a long day at work and sit with mamma in front of the hearth with our feet up, enjoying the peacefulness of the few hours before another round of bombings, where I'd have to rush off again and start my job. I hadn't moved out of mamma's house, but due to the nature of my work, I didn't spend very long there at all. Instead, it was usually just a quick call home so I could sleep and clean up before I was back doing my work. I think my mother silently resented it; she was so used to having an extra pair of hands around to help her that when I was taken away, she didn't quite know how to cope.

I sat up in despair and held my head in my hands before I broke down in tears yet again. It was weird and I wasn't sure how long it was going to take me until I acknowledged that they weren't around anymore, but all I wanted to do was run into mamma's arms and tell her about the awful day I had.

"No! Rose! Don't you dare think like that!" I chastised myself and threw the blanket off of me. "Don't you wallow in self-pity; there are people out there who are suffering worse losses than you!" I walked over to the window and glanced down at the busy street below me. "There are people out there that have absolutely nothing left. You do. Don't you dare get upset!"

I sighed again and wandered around the apartment, getting more and more irate the longer I spoke to myself. "Getting upset isn't going to solve anything; the bastard that did this to you will still be out there!"

"You need to get even. Make sure he doesn't do anything more to hurt the people you care about. You need to fight him!"

I slammed my hands against the wall and made myself jump. I couldn't even begin to think of something that was going to help me get even, but the desire to do so helped me calm down a little.

In an attempt to calm myself down even further, I rummaged in my bag and pulled out a handful of letters from Edward. I had kept them on me, wherever I was, so it felt like I had a piece of him with me all of the time and I really needed to feel him close by at that moment.

I had wrapped most of Edward's letter together with a spare hair ribbon that I'd found lying around my room, but I was surprised to find that there was a loose one. It fluttered to the floor and I realised with excitement that it was one I hadn't opened yet.

With a soft smile, I picked it up off of the floor and stared at it as I held it in my hands. Part of me wanted to open it and read it straight away but another part of me wanted to wait until I was calmer and less distraught. I was also a little worried that it would hold some awful news about an accident he'd been in and I knew that I wasn't going to be able to handle that, in any way, for a long while.

Curiosity won out in the end and with a shaking hand I opened the envelope slowly.

Rosie,

I miss you. I miss you much more than I thought I would.

Every time I look up to the sky and see the stars and the moon I think of you and our time together over Christmas. I send all my prayers to you when I look at those stars Rosie; I just wish I was with you.

Things are scary here, they are frightening and I want to come home. I am fighting for us though; I am fighting for our opportunity to start a life together when I am back.

I received a letter from my mother; it is the first one that she has sent to me. Apparently I have a younger brother, he has just been born. I don't know why she has not told me sooner.

I must go my darling; I need to carry on with my work. Do not forget about me. I will see you soon.

Your love,

Edward.

I resented Edward ever so slightly after reading his letter. At least he still had a mother that could send him letters. I, on the other hand, was left alone in London, living with somebody that I had known for a little less than 6 months and had no family. I didn't know how to get word over to my father or my brother to tell them about the tragedy. At the same time I didn't even know if I still had any family out there that I needed to tell. Nor did I know what was expected of me next. Did I try and arrange a funeral without any attendees or let Pat sort all of that out for me? It was just incredibly unlucky that I happened to see the dead faces of my family and it was because I'd seen them that I didn't know what to do next.

Victoria was another person that I had to tell but I hadn't heard anything from her since mamma had thrown her out back in May and part of me wondered if she'd even care since she was so self-absorbed. The only thing I could think to do was to contact Edward, although I knew that there was absolutely nothing he could do. Either way, I still rummaged around Betty's flat, found some writing paper and sat down to start his letter – the only one I hoped that I'd send this sombre.

Edward,

I miss you too my darling, even more so in the last 24 hours. You see, Swiss Cottage was attacked. The area was destroyed, this includes my entire life. I lost my mother and both of my brothers in that attack! They did not even make it to their fifth birthday! Mamma and I were planning a party for them, with all the kids in the neighbourhood. Oh Edward, you should have seen their faces. They looked so serene and peaceful but at the same time, I have never seen them look so agonisingly painful. I do not know what to do now Edward. I am so scared and alone and I do not know what to do next. Come home to me my darling, come home soon.

All my love,

Your Rose.

I put my pen down and stared at the letter. The longer I thought about the tragedy the angrier I got. I was going to get revenge; one way or another I would get my revenge and destroy Hitler just as he destroyed me. Getting revenge whilst in England was going to be hard but I wasn't going to give up easily. I wasn't going to let Hitler win and I sure as hell wasn't going to let anybody break down against his advances. If the only thing I could do was to keep people happy and cheerful as so much hatred and evil rained down on us, then I was going to make sure that I did it to the best of my capability.

I was going to defeat Hitler before he defeated us.

****

Chapter Nine

Present Day

I stopped talking for a few minutes so I could clear my throat, all the talking was making my mouth dry and I really didn't want to start coughing again. It really hurt my lungs.

As I paused, I looked around the room and was a little shocked by the eager faces staring back at me.

"Aren't you bored?" I muttered and leant over to try and reach my glass of water.

"Ma, why would we be bored?" Elsie took the glass off of the table and handed it to me with a smile. "I told you we like hearing about all this."

I nodded slowly and was relieved as the water seemed to take away the tickle in my throat that was beginning to get annoying.

"I know you do, it's them I'm worried about." I jerked my head in the direction of my seven grandchildren, all of whom were still sat at the end of the bed eagerly watching me. Trent, the eldest at 32, stood up and patted my knee.

"You've never told me this story before, even when I asked you several times..." he leant over and kissed my cheek, "and it's as amazing as I thought it was going to be."

I sighed and shook my head.

"I can't imagine how angry you must've felt..." Trent mumbled as he perched on the side of the bed and took my hand in his. "You're an inspiration you know, you didn't back down."

"Well, I didn't really do much in the end!"

"Mother, don't lie! If you don't tell them how much effort you put into your work, we will." Betty reprimanded from her chair. I rolled my eyes and shuffled around until I was sat up a little more comfortably.

"Shall I carry on then?" I asked skeptically. They all watched me with amused expressions.

"If you don't then we'll bug you with questions until you do Nanna." Trent smiled and moved back to where he was initially sat, which was by my feet with his baby brother, who was 12, on his knee. Michael looked at me with a sad smile and then clapped his hands together.

"What happened next Nanny?" he asked softly. I swallowed back a sudden onslaught of tears as I remember my baby brother who never got to live to his great nephew's age. It killed me to think about how much both my brothers missed out on, how their lives were snatched away at such a tender age.

"Ma, are you all right?" I heard somebody ask me from my side, I nodded my head before squeezing my eyes shut in an attempt to stop the tears.

"Right...where was I?" I asked and inwardly winced as my voice caught and squeaked. I wasn't supposed to still get this upset about their deaths!

"You were telling us about how you were going to get revenge." Suzie chirped.

I nodded and smiled in thanks.

"Right." I sighed, "Well, not much happened throughout 1941. I didn't leave ambulance dispatch, but I made sure I answered as many calls as I could throughout the Blitz. It lasted for 6 months straight; in fact the last major night of was 10th May. By this point, I'd seen some of the most horrific things I'd ever get to see but nobody backed down from the assault."

****

Chapter Ten
1941

The morning after the last major bombing, London woke up properly for the first time in six months. People opened doors slowly and peered out into the streets that were clouded by still settling dust and walked nervously out into the street. We were all a little unsure about whether it had truly finished or not, the air raid siren had sounded but that didn't mean anything, at least, it hadn't over the last couple of nights.

I wandered down into the street, my uniform already on and started to help people that seemed lost or confused in the mess. It took people a while to get used to the fact that it seemed to be over, we couldn't be sure but the final few waves of places had hit like nothing we'd experienced and it had given us all a sense of 'the end'…at least, we hoped it had.

"Rosie? Is that you?" I heard a voice I recognised before I could see the person. The dust hadn't settled much and it was like walking into an incredibly smoky room. I hoped, for my sake, that I wasn't imagining things.

"Rosie? I'm over here!" The shadowy outline of somebody started walking towards me, my heart leapt into my throat when the dust had settled enough for me to see.

"Edward?" I whispered. There was no reason to question it aside from the disbelief that he was actually there. "Is that you?"

He laughed and wrapped his arms around my shoulders, nuzzling his nose into my hair and inhaling.

"Unless you have another Canadian you're expecting, then yes my darling, it is me."

I started crying almost immediately. "How…? How are you here?"

He lent back and wiped my cheeks with the pads of his thumbs.

"I'm on leave."

I nodded and glanced around the street with a frown. "How on earth did you know where I was?"

"I contacted the Ambulance Dispatch."

I laughed humourlessly and shook my head. "They wouldn't give out my details on a whim, how did you do it? "

He kissed my cheek and wrapped his arms back around me. "I told them I was somebody from your family and I had to contact you immediately."

"Oh…"

We stayed in silence for a few minutes as he looked around the street in horror and I kept a check on what was needed of me after he'd gone.

"London…looks…"

"Like the mouth of hell?" I offered with a small shrug. "It has been like this for 6 months now. I've forgotten what it looked like before."

Edward stared at me with wide eyes and a white complexion.

"How are you?"

I shrugged again and stepped away from him so I could quickly help an elderly lady who was stumbling down her garden towards me. I left him stood in the middle of the street as I was bombarded with a series of questions from her before she hobbled back up into her house.

"What was that about?" he asked softly with a small jerk of his head in the direction of her house. I glanced behind me and felt sick when I realised that half of it was missing. I really needed to get her out of there before it caved in on her and she was injured, or worse, killed.

"Where are you going?" he called out to my retreating form. I ignored him for the time being as I tried to walk around the mountains of debris in her garden. "Rose! What are you doing?" He questioned and followed up behind me before grabbing my hand.

"My job!" I hissed and wriggled away from him. I really didn't need any distractions at a time like this considering somebody could get seriously hurt.

"Rose, it isn't safe in there…" he mumbled whilst looking up at the house. I sighed and nodded.

"I know, that's why I need to get her out…"

"What if you get hurt?" He hissed and grabbed for my hand again.

"Edward, I love you, but please let me get her before something does happen!"

He went quiet very quickly and dropped his hand away from me with a stunned look. I frowned before quickly shaking my head and turning my attention back to the task at hand.

"Mrs Simmons, are you there?" I called out as I slowly walked up to the front door, the house was groaning quietly. "Mrs Simmons you need to come out here immediately!" There was no sound from inside the house so I very gently pushed open the front door and fought back the urge to vomit when I saw the inside of the house. The entire back of the building had been ripped away and all that was left was a gaping hole and what appeared to be an unexploded shell. "Mrs Simmons!" I screamed, she tottered around the corner and looked up at me with a squint.

"Yes dear?" she squeaked. I looked at her in a flurry of panic.

"Mrs Simmons, we need to leave here immediately!"

"Why is that dear? Don't you want a cup of tea?"

I shook my head and looked around for her coat and hat. "Mrs Simmons, this house is extremely volatile right now. We must leave immediately!"

She stared up at me with a frown and raised a hand to her mouth in thought. "I don't see the problem young lady; you see Albert is only doing a few repairs at the minute!"

I sighed and looked back at the gaping hole. Albert, her husband, was laying on the floor covered in blood and pieces of wood. He wasn't doing anything.

"I've been living with this for the past week! I don't understand why he doesn't get up off of the floor and carry on working, but that's my Albert for you."

My hand flew up to my mouth and I swallowed back a sob.

"Mrs Simmons…your husband is dead…"

She shook her head and waved her hands about. "Nonsense, Albert is just a heavy sleeper. I've tried waking him but he isn't having any of it. I even made his favourite dinner last night, still couldn't rise him. I think he's deaf."

She laughed a little, "Well, more than he was already. You see, there was an almighty bang in the middle of the night the other week and Albert hasn't been the same since.

I frowned in despair and surveyed the house again. The poor woman didn't understand a thing that was going on.

"Mrs Simmons, shall we go outside the front? I have something to show you."

She looked at me a little nervously. "What is it dear? I'm not very stable in my old age…"

I sighed and looked around again. Her house was a disaster zone and I hated to think about what would happen if I left her in it for any longer. At the same time, I didn't want to stay in it for any longer myself.

"It's the newest…I…" I stared at her dead husband in the kitchen and started shaking. "Mrs Simmons, we need to leave this property immediately."

"Why?" she scrunched her nose up and narrowed her eyes. I sighed; the only way this was going to work was if I ordered her around.

"Mrs Simmons, this house is a dangerous building and at any given moment could collapse. You must evacuate the premises immediately."

"But dear…"

"Mrs Simmons! You must listen to me or I can report you! We need to leave immediately."

***

It took me a further ten minutes but I finally managed to get her out of the house, even if it did mean I had to walk around holding onto the things that she absolutely had to bring and stand there waiting as she told Albert where she was going. I managed to contact somebody at the local ARP station and got them to look after her whilst I let Betty know the state of the house. Within the hour the house was cornered off and a bomb disposal team was on its way.

It was only then that I remember Edward was around. I spun around in the street in a panic in case he'd left without saying goodbye, but found him standing in a peculiarly similar position to what I'd left him in. I wandered over with a small smile.

"Is everything okay?" I questioned when he didn't say anything to me. "You look really pale…"

He still didn't answer me.

"Edward?" I stood directly in front of him and silently cursed the height difference; I was pretty much jumping up and down to get his attention by the time he looked at me.

"Oh! Sorry, I was thinking…"

I sighed and rubbed the bridge of my nose. "You've been thinking for a while now."

He looked down at me with a massive grin.

"Edward…is everything okay?" I repeated nervously. His moods were slightly intimidating, especially when he seemed to jump from completely silent and thoughtful to incredibly happy in a heartbeat.

"You said you loved me."

I paled and my body flooded with cold fear. "I…did?"

He nodded enthusiastically. "Yes! You said it just before you went into the house."

"Oh…"

I looked down at my feet in embarrassment and bit my lip in fear. I hadn't planned on saying it until he'd said it first, I was scared that I was being too abrupt and forward but because I'd been focusing on Mrs Simmons, it just slipped out and I wasn't prepared for any flak I was about to get because of it.

"You're wincing…" he whispered as he gently held onto my chin and forced me to look up at him. "You're wincing and your blush is adorable." He mumbled in the same breath. I relaxed my face and sighed.

"Sorry."

"Why are you wincing?" he questioned as he stepped closer to me.

"I'm just…nervous?" I shrugged and tried to move my head so I wasn't staring at him.

"Don't you dare hide from me…" he muttered and moved us so we were standing inappropriately close for the middle of the street. I tried to move away from him again but his arm had locked me into place. His gaze flickered from my eyes to my lips and back again. He grinned.

"I love you." He pressed his lips against my forehead. "I love you." He muttered again with a kiss to my nose. "I" he pressed a kiss to one cheek, "love" he kissed my other cheek, "you!" he laughed before pressing his mouth against mine.

***

We were laughing and joking as I led him back to Betty's flat, he hadn't stopped whispering how much he loved me but I hadn't said it since.

"Where are we going?" Edward asked softly when I lead him up to the door.

"Home…" I shrugged and knocked to see if Betty was home. When she didn't answer I let myself in and called out to her. We'd devised a code to let each other know that we were coming home if other people were with us and we weren't decent. The amount of times we'd been caught in our nighties or underwear was ridiculous. Most of the Ambulance Dispatch had now seen us in varying states of undress.

"Blackbird's home?" I called out. Edward looked at me in amusement and concern at the same time.

90

"Blackbird! Blackbird!" I heard come from her room and stalled in the hallway.

"What's going on…?" Edward asked with a laugh, I held my finger to his lips before I said anything so I could hear Betty's answer.

"Blackbird safe!"

I laughed at the expression on Edward's face and walked him into the flat. "Welcome to my new home." I muttered sourly. It wasn't anything impressive and my room, at the back of the flat, was about the size of a cupboard but I couldn't complain because Betty had made sure that I had everything I needed after I'd been thrown head first into a family tragedy.

Edward nodded and wound his arm around my waist as he dropped a kiss to the top of my head. "I'm sorry I wasn't here for you…"

I nodded in acknowledgement and smiled softly at him. "It's all right, you didn't know."

"So, who is the lucky soldier you've brought back today then?" Betty chirped as she walked out of her room and came to see me. I paled and started shaking my head emphatically. Her step faltered when she realised that for the first time I was stood next a guy and it wasn't just a work friend. She recovered quickly and turned on the charm.

"So, who is this handsome fellow?" she questioned and thrust her hand out in front of her.

"Betty, this is Edward." I paused and looked pointedly at her. "Edward, this is Betty."

As they exchanged pleasantries and he kissed her on the cheek she threw me a look of surprise, apology and approval. I waited until what she'd shouted dawned on her and giggled when I watched the colour drain from her face.

"Oh! I think I should clear things up and clarify that you're the only man she's ever brought here. You're the only man she's ever talking about."

I quickly turned to face Edward and blushed when he winked at us both. "She was expecting a different Canadian earlier anyway; I wouldn't be surprised if that was a lie."

Betty grinned and elbowed me in the side. "He's funny, keep him around will'ya?"

I sighed, shook my head and looked down at the floor, "Why do I have the feeling that the rest of the day will be spent laughing at my expense?"

Betty rolled her eyes, "because it will!"

***

Thankfully she had to head to work pretty soon after we'd gotten back and it then dawned on me that I was supposed to be joining her.

"Edward…I have to get to work…" I mumbled and looked around the flat for my hat. Betty grabbed my hand and took me back to the living room before quite roughly shoving me down on the chair.

"I'm your boss, I decide whether you have to be in or not and right now you're not needed."

"But!" I was about to start complaining, I'd been trying to work up the ranks so I was on the same level as her and missing a day off work wasn't going to help me.

"Darling, you're already a senior officer, just enjoy the day off!"

I sighed and rolled my eyes at her back as she left the flat. Edward cleared his throat.

"So, care to enlighten me on the whole Blackbird thing?" He smiled at me and crossed the room so he could kneel next to the chair I was sat in.

"It's just...something we do, so we can let each other know if we're dressed or not when somebody else is with us." I shrugged and closed my eyes. "I'm so happy you're here right now."

I peered over at him and frowned at the sad look on his face. He took my hands in his and started to bite the inside of his lip. I really didn't like the way things seemed to be going.

"Rosie...darling...I really am here to give you some news about your family."

I went cold with fear again before screwing my eyes shut and shaking my head.

"I was in France... with your father." Edward spoke softly and I tried to focus on what he was saying but all I could really hear was the blood rushing around in my head. I felt his hands squeeze mine and opened my eyes to looks at him.

"Rose, I need you to focus. I need you to hear what I'm about to say."

I nodded slowly and my heart sank. I knew what the next words out of his mouth were going to be.

"Rosie, your father is dead."

I stared at him is disbelief. This was incredibly unfair. First my mother and brothers and now my father had been taken? I shook my head slowly "How...how do you know?"

Edward sighed, sat on the floor and very delicately pulled me onto his lap so I could cuddle into him. "Darling, I saw him get shot. We didn't notice the Jerry who had snuck up behind us. I saw him get shot..."

I started crying again. I hated this war. Hated the man that had caused it and hated how much it had taken from me.

"He died in my arms..." Edward whispered brokenly and started to rock me in an attempt to quieten me down. "He died in my arms..."

"My…my brother?" I asked through a heaving sob.

"Prisoner of War."

I cried harder. My entire family had been ripped away from me because of some power-hungry dictator and his stupid war. Edward stayed quiet for a little while longer before pressing a kiss to my forehead and my temple when I calmed down enough to stop shaking.

"Your father wanted me to tell you that he loved you so very much and he's very proud of his little girl." He paused and hushed me as I started to whimper. "I told him everything that you were doing, I kept him up to date with everything, he was so proud of you." Edward whispered and smiled sadly, "The day he found out he'd lost his wife and sons he went out and killed 30 people. I've never seen a man so bloodthirsty. Your father was one of a kind Rosie and so are you."

He took my hands in his again and kissed the palms. "He told me one other thing before he took his last breath…"

I chanced a glance up at Edward's face and saw that his own eyes had filled with tears.

"He told me to marry you the instance I could because I was going to lose something extremely special if I didn't…"

I gave him a watery smile and nodded.

"Rosie, marry me tomorrow?"

I gasped and stared at him in amazement as he rummaged around his uniform for a small ring.

"It isn't much but I bought it when I could in France…"

I smiled softly and nodded.

"Yes." I pecked him. "Yes!"

∗∗∗

Waking up on the morning of May 12th was a strange experience. Instead of rolling out of bed groggily and hating the fact that it was another day, I jumped out of bed in excitement and anticipation. Edward was back and I was getting married. Betty had managed to sort out the impossible – again – and had our ceremony at the Town Hall scheduled for 1 in the afternoon. My joy was somewhat short lived as I   remembered my tragedies but I tried my hardest to push that into the back of my mind for the duration of the day.

***

"Rose, I pulled enough strings to get you this time – please don't be late."

Betty started shouting at me through the door. It was just after 12 so I still had plenty of time, even if she thought I didn't. I rolled my eyes and carried on trying to sort my hair out. I'd let it out of its usual bun and had pinned the sides back but it just wasn't staying in the right place.

"Rose! Seriously! It's nearly half 12…"

I sighed and opened the door, blowing a wisp of hair out of my face. "Betty I look terrible! I can't turn up to my own wedding looking like this…"

Betty shook her head in amusement and pinned the loose strand of hair back for me. "Rose stop being silly, you don't look terrible."

I turned back to my mirror and narrowed my eyes at my reflection. When I'd joined the Ambulance Dispatch, we were issued two uniforms – a navy blue one for everyday use and a white one with gold lining for important events. Since I'd lost all my formal clothes when Swiss Cottage was bombed, I'd opted for the white suit as my wedding outfit. I smoothed down the skirt and started picking off imaginary bits of lint that I thought I could see.

"Rose, you look lovely! Stop faffing around and let's go before you miss the slot or Edward thinks you've left him."

With a resigned sigh and one more fluff of my hair, I turned to leave. "I'm going to make him buy me a wedding dress next time."

***

After several weeks of rain and grey cloud, the sun was shining down on us. The Town Hall was only 5 minutes away but we decided to take a slight detour to pick up some flowers for Betty and I, which resulted in a lovely walk in the spring sunshine. When we arrived – only a few minutes late – Edward was pacing outside nervously.

"There you are!" He ran down the steps and clutched my hand, bringing it up to his mouth to press a kiss there. "I thought you'd gotten hurt or you weren't going to turn up! You really panicked me there…"

I laughed and kissed him on his cheek. "Don't be silly, I just didn't know what to wear…"

Edward grinned at me and pulled me towards him for a hug. "You look wonderful Rosie, you always do."

I blushed and ducked my head in embarrassment. Betty elbowed me in the ribs and mouthed 'I told you so'. Edward watched me for a few minutes with a small smile on his face. "Ready to become Mrs McGraw?" He winked at me and wound his arm around my waist.

"More than you'll ever know."

***

"Dearly beloved we are gathered here today…"

I suppressed a giggle as the registrar started his spiel. The 'dearly beloved' that were gathered was literally Betty and Pat – they were the only people that could come with us on such short notice, especially considering all the people Edward wanted were either still fighting or in Canada. I smiled lovingly up at Edward as the registrar carried on talking – it was a complete whirlwind romance but I couldn't think of another place I wanted to be at that exact moment. Although I was blissfully happy, it still hurt that I didn't have mamma, father or any of my brothers with me but knowing that my father had given Edward his blessing was enough to dull the pain.

The registrar stopped speaking for a short moment to turn the page he was reading when he was cut off by an air raid siren that started wailing in the distance. I sighed and counted the seconds until the rest of London picked up the screeching chorus.

"What is that?" Edward muttered as the sound steadily got louder.

"Air Raid Siren. We need to find a shelter." I looked around the room quickly and spotted the exit and was about to lead everybody away when the registrar shoved a piece of paper under our noses.

"Sign that! Sign it quickly and get out of here! Save yourself." I grabbed a pen from the table before quickly signing the license. As soon as Edward had scrawled his name, the registrar clapped his hands together.

"Congratulations, you are now husband and wife! The closest shelter is the basement of the building." With that he sprinted out of the door with Edward hot on his heels.

"What about work?" I muttered as Betty, Pat and I scurried out of the building.

"We'll go, you go back to your husband."

I shook my head and opened the door to the ambulance that had just pulled up. "No, I'm not missing work. They need me."

Pat grabbed my arms and pushed me back towards the entrance to the Town Hall. "Your husband needs you. *Edward* needs you. Go before you get yourself killed."

I narrowed my eyes at them and went to argue against their decision. "It's my jo-"

Pat shook his head. "As of this moment we no longer need your services. Your job is that of a wife. Go."

****

Chapter Eleven

Present Day

"You lost your father, your job and your wedding was cut short because of a bombing?" Trent asked in disbelief. I nodded slowly and wiped the tears away from my eyes. Thinking about everything was entirely too upsetting. "How did you cope?"

"The only choice I had was to cope. The following day after the wedding, Pat gave me my job back and I guess the news of my father's death was blunted by the fact Edward proposed immediately afterwards." I shook my head to clear my thoughts; things were beginning to get a little fuzzy.

"Are there any pictures of your wedding?" Suzie asked with a bright smile, I was grateful that she had managed to change the topic.

"Somewhere. I'm not entirely sure where though, you'll have to look around."

Betty laughed, "I remember seeing a picture of you and dad looking terrified outside a building, I'd always wondered what was going on."

I smiled at everybody and sighed happily, "I think in the end, Edward and I ended up getting married three times and I never regretted one of them! I was just grateful he bought me a dress the second time."

There was a small silence in the room.

"Just think, if you weren't forced to that dance, you wouldn't have met the man of your dreams." Trent mused, "and we wouldn't all be sat here listening to you tell us about how it was." He smiled softly at me. "Nanna, I'm so proud of you."

I raised an eyebrow and cocked my head to the left slightly.

"You're proud…?"

He nodded and patted my knee. "Yes, because you have this unbelievable strength about you." Everybody else started nodding in agreement. I continued to lay there extremely confused. Flattered, but confused.

"I do…?"

Trent rolled his eyes. "Nanna, nobody I know has had to deal with the death of their entire family and has lived to tell the story 70 years later."

I smiled at him and laughed, "Trent my boy, you don't know anybody else that's this old."

There was a little round of laughter and then Trent cleared his throat.

"I know, but what I mean is that…" he paused and scratched the back of his head. "I mean that… you…" he coughed uncomfortably. "Can't you just accept that I'm proud?"

I laughed again and nodded, "Yes, I suppose I can. Though I'm sure we brought you up to be able to articulate what you're thinking…" I teased and grinned when he blushed.

"It's difficult when you're being put on the spot!" He argued. I started giggling.

"You see! This is why I'm sat here feeling a little intimidated by the fact you want to know all of this."

There was silence in the room again, I sighed and leant back against the pillows. Suzie cleared her throat and turned her watery eyes on me. "We want to know because it's a part of your life that we'll never know unless you tell us." She paused and glanced around the room, "and we don't know..." she bit her lip. "We don't know how long you have left to tell us."

I was about to say something when Betty spoke over me. "It wasn't her entire family."

There was a moment when everybody turned to her confused, she laughed and ran a hand through her hair. "Sorry, I was thinking about what Trent said. You hadn't lost everybody there had you? Your brother was still a Prisoner of War..."

I nodded and thought back to it. "You're right. He was still around then."

"What happened to him then?" Trent asked softly. I started at him before averting my gaze onto the back of the wall.

"He managed to escape. I'll never truly figure out how he did it."

"He escaped? Wasn't he in occupied France though?"

I nodded my head slowly, "Yes. I think he managed to get over to America.

They turned to face me with wide eyes,

"How on earth did he manage that?"

I laughed a little, "My brother was apparently surprisingly good at sneaking around."

Elsie coughed lightly, "Why haven't we ever met your bother Ma?"

I shrugged, "We fell out of contact back in the 50s at some point, when both of you were still quite young."

"Did he not try to make contact throughout the years?"

"No...I believe I heard about him getting married in the 80s, but it could have been anyone. John was a popular name back then."

"Do you miss him?" she asked softly.

"I miss each and every single one of them."

Betty got up and walked over to the window so she could close the blind. "Ma, was I named after your friend?"

I watched her in amusement, "It's taken you how many years to ask me that?"

She shrugged and sat back down, "You've never told us this story with so much detail. I didn't realise how close you two were."

I reached out and took both of my daughters' hands. "You're both named after people who were very special to me." They waited for me to clarify what I meant. I turned to Betty.

"Yes, you were named after my friend. She was – well still is – incredibly important to me. She was the only one there for me during that part of my life and she's been like a big sister since." I turned to face Elsie.

"And you, my darling, were named after my mother. Elsie Elizabeth Wren, although most people just called her Beth."

"What happened next?" Michael asked me from around the thumb that he'd been sucking for a while. It was a habit that he'd had since he'd been born and was apparently one that he wasn't going to break any time soon.

"Well, I started to travel the country." I paused for a second as I tried to remember all the details of my little tour of the country. "Although the bombing had stopped in London, they didn't stop attacking the country and I fought hard against Ma'am and Betty to be given the opportunity to go and help."

✳✳✳✳

Chapter Twelve
1941

"Why can't I go?" I hissed in annoyance at Betty as she shook her head for the thousandth time.

"I'm not losing you to another part of the country Rose, you're too important here!"

I slammed my hands on the desk and stared at her dead in the eyes. "You don't *understand* Betty, there's nothing I can do here right now. I *need* to go and help! I have to!"

Betty sighed, rubbed her eyes and closed the book she was making notes in. She turned her tired eyes up to me and linked her fingers in front of her.

"I know you think you have to avenge the souls of your family, or something like that, but you don't have to do it 1000 miles away from here!"

I walked across the room to the lone chair lent up against the wall and fell into it with an exhausted huff.

"You don't understand."

"You've already said that Rose. I know why you want to do it, I get that – seriously I do. There is just no practicality behind it."

"Betty…"

She stood up and walked the short distance between us so she could stand in front of my chair.

"Rose, what happens if something starts in London again? We *need* you *here*. You're far too important to lose."

"But…"

"Rose, I'm not going to give you permission."

I jumped up from the chair in annoyance and screamed in frustration. Betty had fast become something of an enemy, especially when she wanted to keep me away from helping people.

"London can survive without me." I hissed and rounded on her. "I have nothing left here. I have nothing left to do here."

Betty bit her lip and started looking down at the floor.

"I'm going to go whether you like it or not, but I'd prefer I had you on board."

"Why are you being like this Rose? Why don't you get that I need you here?"

I rolled my eyes and perched on the edge of the table whilst trying my hardest to calm my ever-rising temper.

"Betty, I'm replaceable. There is somebody out there that can do my job as good – or even better – than me. I'm going with the officers in the morning."

"Rose…"

I waved my hand to quieten her and gave her a small smile before leaving the room. I had to start getting ready if I was to leave in the morning. She followed me and grabbed my arm, I sighed and was getting ready to give her a hundred more reasons as to why I was going when she shoved a piece of paper in my hand.

"Be safe."

***

Betty had once again tried to convince me to not go when she got home later that night, but I completely ignored anything she had to say to me. In fact, at one point I was mere seconds away from leaving the flat and staying at Pat's for the night because it was getting too hard to handle.

"What would Edward say about this?"

I looked at her before shaking my head vigorously. "You're not going to get me to not go by bringing him up."

"Rose, he's your husband. You can't leave him!"

I dropped what was in my hands back onto the bed and placed them firmly against my hips. "He left me first! He's the one out there fighting!"

"He had no choice! What do you think he's going to say when he knows you're putting yourself in danger?"

"He'd tell me that he was proud I was doing something with my anger." I retorted and turned my back on her. A couple of seconds later I felt her touch the small of my back as she tried to stop me from packing.

"Please think about this…" she pleaded. Her eyes were bright with unshed tears.

"I have Betty. I've not stopped thinking about it."

"Where do you go first?" Betty muttered a few minutes later, I could tell by the look on her face that she was admitting defeat and I was free to go.

"Well, I think we're going to Norwich first, we're needed to help with the clean – up."

Betty nodded and turned to leave my room. "Just, let me know when you get there."

***

If I was going to be honest with myself, I knew that I didn't really want to be travelling around the country when there was a very possible chance that another wave of bombing could start up at any minute. Yet, given my desire to get revenge in any way that I could, I was the first person waiting at the bus the next morning. Pat turned up not long after me and handed over an itinerary.

"This is where we're going for the next little while." He muttered, his voice gruff with sleep. I took the sheet from him and stared down at the four names. They'd all be hit several times before our last major raid on the 10th, but it had taken until now, the 18th, for the call for help to reach London. I glanced back up at Pat with a frown.

"How bad is it?"

He shrugged and climbed into the driver's seat. "I don't know duck, if they're still trying to clean up now then it could be horrendous."

I nodded and looked back down at my sheet; there was a very probable chance that I was making a very big mistake.

***

As it turned out, the mess wasn't as bad as we had prepared ourselves for – though they hadn't prepared themselves much for any type of raid considering everyone expected it to be down in London. It took us a week but we managed to help sort out the chaos in every place on our sheet and by the time I was back in London, back in the flat, I was exhausted but happy.

We weren't called out again until the beginning of June. Canterbury had suffered a night of bombing and needed our help immediately. We understood why it was so urgent when we arrived, everywhere I looked there was a fire or a burnt out building. Houses were still collapsing and there were wounded

106

people lying around everywhere. It was early morning when we got there.

"Rose, you need to get out of this bus immediately and get to that family at the other side of the street." Pat shouted as he jumped out of the door, I looked up from my clipboard and looked at the family he was talking about. There were three people stood there, each of them were younger than the age of 10. I swallowed harsh, sighed and gave myself a quick pep talk. I hopped out of the bus and calmly made my way over there, I didn't want to make them any more nervous than they appeared to be.

"Hello, my name is Rose…what's yours?" I crouched down to their level and turned my attentions to the tallest child. He eyed me nervously and put his arms around his siblings before narrowing his eyes.

"Robert…" he muttered and then looked down at the children in his arms, "this is my brother and sister…" he whispered. I looked over at them and smiled gently, the little girl started wailing, broke away from her brother and threw her arms around my neck. I could feel the grime all over her body and knew that I was going to be completely covered in a matter of minutes. Her little brother also latched himself onto my neck and started to cry. I glanced over at Robert and frowned, he looked like he was about to start crying too.

I stood up quickly and glanced around the street to find them somewhere they could go and warm up but there wasn't much left standing. Pat saw me looking around and waved me back over to the bus.

"Robert, follow me." He nodded and kept close to my side as I held his crying brother and sister. Pat immediately took the boy from my arms and rocked him a little to try and calm him.

We got them into the back of the bus and covered them all in blankets before giving them something to drink and a piece of bread each.

"What happened?" I asked softly. The little girl screwed her eyes shut again and started to shake her head. Robert looked at me with wide eyes and started to talk to me through his mouthful of bread.

"There was a loud noise coming from the street so mummy ran outside to see what was going on…" he chewed a little more before swallowing and tearing off another mouthful. "She started screaming at me, John and Polly to stay inside but I went outside anyway."

I nodded encouragingly and kept stroking Polly's matted brown hair as she cried softly into my chest. "What happened next…?" I pushed gently; Robert turned his big brown eyes up at me and shivered.

"There was this really bright light and then a very loud bang." He paused and looked out of the window at the street. "Mummy just disappeared…I started calling her name but I don't know where she went…"

He sniffled a little and then carried on talking, "I found part of her coat in the street though but I don't know where she went. Everything was dusty and black and it was scary."

I reached out and wiped a tear that was making its way down his grimy face. "Where were Polly and John when this happened?" I asked him slowly. He bit his lip.

"I know mummy said to stay inside, but I took Polly with me. I didn't want her to get upset and scared on her own. I needed to look after her."

I nodded, "How old are you Robert?"

He puffed his little chest in pride. "I'm six."

"How old are John and Polly?" I glanced back at Pat and smiled when I noticed that John had fallen asleep in his arms. Pat's eyes were filled with tears and it shocked me. I hadn't seen him cry at any point during our work.

"John is four…" I swallowed down the threat of tears, the poor little boy.

"Po is the baby. She's only two."

With wide eyes I looked down at Polly. It broke my heart that these children had to deal with such horror at such a young age. Pat cleared his throat and spoke quietly to Robert. "Why weren't you in the countryside with the cows and fields?"

Robert frowned and shook his head, "we were but mummy didn't like it without us so she came and got us."

Pat nodded and gently laid John down on the front seat before grabbing his clipboard and making some notes.

"When is mummy coming back?" Robert whispered with a heartbroken face. My eyes darted to Pat; he shrugged and mouthed 'Tell him'. I took a shuddering breath.

"She…she won't be coming back darling." The look on his face could have made even the most steely of men cry.

"Why…?"

I bit my lip and tried to think of the most appropriate way to answer his question. "Sometimes when somebody is really needed in Heaven, God takes them."

He nodded his head slowly. "Mummy told me about Heaven, she told me that Rudy went there."

"Who was Rudy?"

"He was our dog, he got really sick last year."

I let Robert carry on telling me about his dog whilst Pat whispered some information to me. Apparently, according to a couple of their neighbours, a bomb had landed in the middle of the street but hadn't exploded. When Robert's mother had realised what it was, she was screaming at her children to stay inside. It was when she walked backwards and knocked the bomb that it exploded. Thankfully the children were not anywhere near enough to get hurt majorly by the blast but they had been knocked over and the front windows of the houses in the street had imploded.

I gasped and covered my mouth when I realised what it meant Robert had really seen, the only good thing that I could pick up on was the fact his mother didn't suffer. It didn't mean much to anybody right at that moment however, we were consoling three children and didn't know what we were supposed to do next.

"I'll see if anybody knows if they have any other family." Pat whispered and quickly walked away from the bus, leaving me with two sleeping children and an animated little boy.

***

"What happened to those children then?" Betty asked worriedly as we sat in our favourite café sipping coffee during a lunch break.

"One of the neighbours knew their family in the country and they were shipped out there again."

Betty nodded and swirled the liquid around in her cup. "That must have been horrible…"

I nodded and stared down at my hands on the table, "I don't think I'm ever going to fully recover from that. That little boy was so heartbroken, it sort of makes me glad that both my brothers were killed with Mamma."

Betty raised an eyebrow, "Sorry?"

"I don't know what I would've done if Michael or David were left alone without Mamma. They'd have been distraught."

Betty sighed and patted my hand, "Well, you don't need to think about that do you?"

110

I shook my head and stared out over the street. "No, I suppose I don't. I just can't believe that they've gone."

****

Chapter Thirteen

1942

The devastation of war started to peter out by the end of 1941 and the beginning of 1942. Pearl Harbour had been attacked in December by the Japanese and that had caused America to enter the war, a feat that they'd not managed up until this point and it let everybody relax just a little. We were surely going to win with the help of the Americans.

My brother had managed to escape the Prisoner of War camp and had sent me a telegram to let me know that he was okay, though I didn't hear anything else from him for long stretches of time. He was apparently on the run around France, trying to keep away from occupied streets and towns and pretending to be German if it was the only thing he could do.

My life started to return to normal after I came back from Canterbury. I was beginning to accept the loss of my parents and baby brothers and I was beginning to accept that my husband wasn't going to be around for a while. We kept in contact through letters as often as we could, but they were beginning to become far and few between. Betty and I soon thought about leaving ambulance dispatch when we'd had enough of Ma'am and didn't think we were going to be needed any time soon, though we informed Pat to get into contact with the both of us the instance they needed us back, which in truth was only a couple of times. It only took a couple of weeks before we were bored again and begged for our jobs back.

**

"Rose! Get up!"

I heard Betty screech and before I could entirely understand what was going on, she had barged into my room, grabbed my arm and dragged me out of the door.

"You need to get to the front door this second!" she hissed and pushed me towards the living room. I started to fight against her when I realised how indecent I was.

"I'm not even dressed…" I hissed and then grabbed a hold of the corner of the wall.

"I don't think that matters right now."

"What is it anyway?" I asked when she ran into my room and grabbed my robe. She looked at me with a frown before she quickly informed me that there were two uniformed officers standing on the doorstep saying they had to talk to me urgently.

"Why didn't you tell me that straight away!?" I shrieked and ran to the door. Betty muttered something at my retreating form but I chose to ignore her as I ran at the two officers.

"Please God No. Please God No." I rounded the corner and saw the sombre faces of the two men stood at the door.

"Please God No. PLEASE GOD NO!" I chanted hysterically, my entire body shaking with fear. "Not Edward *anybody* but Edward. Please…"

They cleared their throats and took their hats off before bowing to me and keeping their gaze solidly on my face. I tightened my robe around me and waited for them to say something, my mouth was getting extremely dry.

The taller man of the two blinked his green eyes a couple of times before clearing his throat again and sighing.

"Ma'am, are you Mrs McGraw?"

I nodded quickly, "Yes, is there a problem officer?" My voice came out much more level than I was expecting.

"We have some news regarding your husband."

I knew that's what they were there for and it was beginning to annoy me that they were drawing out the inevitable.

"What's happened?" I snapped and quickly smiled apologetically.

"There has been an accident. Edward was caught up in a cross fire and was shot."

I felt the colour drain from my face and jumped slightly when I felt Betty come up behind me and hook her arm through mine.

"Is he...Is he...dead?" I questioned slowly, the room was beginning to spin.

There was a short silence before either officer answered, it didn't help calm me down, instead I spent the time panicking that he was gone forever and I hadn't seen him since we'd married.

"No, but there is another problem."

I breathed a sigh of relief, at least he was still alive.

"And that is?"

"He's been sent back to Canada and isn't able to come back to England."

There were another few seconds of silence as what they'd said sunk in.

"What!?" I shouted. They flinched slightly and handed me over a letter.

"He can't get over to England, it isn't safe enough."

"Well when can he?"

"When the war has ended ma'am…"

I looked over at Betty with wide eyes; she returned the look with a frown.

"When the war has *ended*?" I questioned in disbelief. They nodded slowly.

"When the *war* has *ended*?" They gave each other a concerned look and nodded again.

"*When* the *war* has ENDED?" I repeated with a scream. They stepped back in shock.

"Ma'am you need to calm down!"

I hissed at them and narrowed my eyes, "You do not get to come into my house, tell me my husband is stuck in Canada until the *end of the war* and then tell me to calm down."

They shuffled around on their feet; Betty sighed and led me away from the door before sending them away with several apologies and a thank you for delivering the news. I had sat down on the chair and was still ranting about it.

"How is this fair?" I questioned Betty when she came into the room with a cup of tea.

"I don't know Rose…" she gave me a small shrug and handed the cup over to me.

"I've lost my mother, my brothers and my father and now my husband is injured in CANADA!"

Betty patted my back and hummed in agreement. "I know Rose, I know."

I sighed and shook my head, "I don't know what to do anymore."

There was a short silence as I thought about my options.

"Betty…?" I paused and waited until she turned to face me, "Do you think I could get over to Canada?"

Betty frowned and then shook her head slowly, "If they can't get over to England, what makes you think you can get over there?"

I tapped the edge of the table with my nail, "Didn't you just send a group of officers to America the other day?"

She looked at me incredulously, "They were requested though. Why?"

I laughed happily when I realised that my plan could come together. "I'm a trained nurse as well as a Captain, surely you can think of something to get me sent over there for?"

Betty sighed and sat down on the chair opposite me.

"What is it with you and asking me to do the impossible?" she muttered through the gap in her hands as she rested her head in them.

"The impossible is always possible." I smiled a little and mentally noted that I needed to write to Edward before anything could be confirmed.

"Not when you're asking me to find reasons for you to go to Canada. It was hard enough getting them for you to travel around the country!"

"Yes, and who was in the news because of it?" I retorted, she rolled her eyes and shook her head again. The story about the three children had been picked up by the locals news and whilst I was in Canterbury helping with the following bombings, both my name and Pat's had been plastered across the headlines.

"Rose, you do realise that this is going to be nigh on impossible…right?"

I nodded and swallowed hard. "Try though, please try. I can't bear to think about Edward alone in Canada injured."

Betty patted my arm and smiled softly, "He's going to be with his family..."

"But not his wife!"

***

Edward

Two officers came to the house this morning, they gave me your Canadian address. I thought they were going to tell me that you had been killed but I was so relieved that it was only an injury! Although, I am not happy you are injured, just happy you are not dead. Betty is going to try and sort something out for us darling, Blackbird is coming home.

I love you,

Yours forever,

Rosie.

I'd initially told him that I was planning on travelling over to him and looking after him until we both could return to England, but Betty have very quickly and rightly reminded me that it would be incredibly dangerous for everyone if the letter go intercepted. I panicked for a while until I remembered that I'd told him the meaning behind the little code that Betty and I had, and since he'd taken to calling me his 'little blackbird' I thought it was fitting.

"Is this going to be okay?" I asked whilst I waved the letter in Betty's face. She grabbed at it and read through it quickly with a hum.

"Yes, I suppose that will do. Now hurry up and get that sent, I can't do anything until I know Edward knows."

I nodded quickly and quickly ran out of the flat, skipping through the streets to the local post office.

***

Trying to get the higher powers to let me travel out to Canada when it was going to be extremely dangerous, was harder than I had expected. Betty was stood on the side lines pushing as much as she could but I could see the 'I told you so' smile that kept plastering itself on her face. During the two weeks where I spent numerous amounts of hours arguing my case, I'd received a series of letters from Edward. They steadily changed their tone and by the time I'd managed to get my way, he was on board with the idea.

Rosie,

Darling, I am fine. I wish you were not going to do this though; I will be ever so worried about you. I must admit, I cannot wait until I have you in my arms, but I will wait until the end of the war if I have to. I want you to be safe my darling, I do not want anything to happen to you. I suppose that there is nothing I can say that will change your mind, considering you have ignored every other letter I have sent on this subject. So I will see you when I see you my little blackbird. Home is waiting.

Yours for always,

Edward.

I waited nervously outside the door of Ma'am's office, as she, Betty, Pat and an elderly gentleman with a name I could never remember, talked about my demands. The instance I heard chairs shuffling and the squeak of the door opening, I felt sick. They were going to, in a matter of minutes, either destroy my world or build it up.

"Mrs McGraw, please explain once again why you feel you are needed in Canada." Ma'am spoke gruffly and jerked her head at the chair in front of the table. "Sit."

I nodded quickly and made my way over to my seat before I said the words that I had been practicing for days.

"I feel that I need to be over in Canada to help with the injured soldiers. They have done everything they can to support Britain in her bid to win the war, the least we can do is send some of our officers over there to help them."

"Do you not think that they already have their own helping them?"

I blushed in fear and ducked my head slightly. Ma'am never liked it if you looked her in the eyes, but looking down was just as bad.

"Look at me when I'm speaking to you, young lady!"

I snapped my attention back to the wall directly above her head and folded my hands onto my lap. "There isn't much that we, as a country, can do for anywhere in the world just yet." I took a deep breath and tried to unscramble the words that were muddled up in my head.

"Yes?" Ma'am snapped. I sighed, I wasn't going to help myself much by lying about my true intentions. I was sure Betty had already told them and I knew Ma'am had a heart, even if she didn't like to show if very often.

"My husband is stuck over in Canada, injured, and I'd very much like the opportunity to go over there and be with him whilst helping him heal."

Ma'am nodded and scribbled something down on the paper in front of her. "What makes you think that we're going to let you go?"

I shrugged and smiled slightly. "I just hope that you all realise how important this is for me. Especially since I lost my entire family and he's all I have left."

Betty made a weird whimpering noise from the corner of the room and very quickly left before anybody could ask her what was wrong. Ma'am frowned.

"Everybody has lost members of their family…" she spat. I gritted my teeth and forced myself to be polite. I wasn't going to get anywhere if I just started shouting at her.

"I know and my heart goes out to each and every single one of them, but Ma'am…I lost all family I had to the war. I'm completely on my own now and I couldn't handle it if I lost my husband while he was so far away from me."

There was silence throughout the room; I didn't know what to do so I just carried on talking.

"I'm a registered nurse; I can work with one of the stations out there. I know how to drive an ambulance, so I'm helpful there too. I wouldn't be going over to Canada and then not help in the war effort. I just wish to be with my husband because I have nothing left here in London."

I chanced a look at Ma'am and saw that her eyes had filled with tears. She coughed to clear her throat and handed me a slip of paper.

"You need training before you go, in case something happens to you out at sea."

She abruptly stood up from the table and left the room. I stared at her back in amazement.

***

Silence fell across the room as the door opened and quickly slammed shut when Ma'am stormed out. I stared at Pat in wonder.

"Did I just…?" I questioned with a frown and pointed out the door. He nodded and wiped under his eyes.

"Yes, it appears that you just did." He laughed and clasped my shoulder. "You never cease to amaze me, duck. You're a wonder."

I smiled up at him, "I'll take that as a compliment."

"It wasn't intended in any other way. I'll go get Betty."

I stood up and went to follow him out of the room, "Is she okay?"

"You have a very moving story duck, but at the same time I think she's scared you're going to forget about her."

I sighed and laughed softly, "Silly cow. Send her to my office. I'll talk some sense into her."

"Will do duck."

I smiled and clucked my tongue as I remembered something else I needed to say. "Oh, and Pat? Thanks for sticking up for me."

He grinned and wandered out of the room, leaving me standing in the centre of it, shaking but wholly amazed that I was allowed to go.

***

Betty came into my office with a very drawn face and red eyes that were obviously puffy from crying.

"I heard that she let you go..." she whispered brokenly. I nodded and walked around the table to give her a hug.

"Why are you so upset?"

Betty shrugged and buried her head in my arm. "I'm not, I just have a cold."

I hugged her for a few minutes before laughing softly, "I saw you dart out of the room earlier Betty, what's bothering you?"

She shook her head and perched on the edge of the desk. "It's just how strong you are. I'm amazed; I just wish that I was that strong."

I frowned and watched her intently, it didn't seem like I was going to get her to tell me what was wrong easily.

I handed her a cup of tea that I'd made on my way back to the room.

"Betty, I've been living with you for the past 2 years, I know you better than this. What's bothering you?"

She took the mug from me with shaking hands and brushed a stray piece of hair out of her face with a sigh. "It's ridiculous really..."

"Nothing is ridiculous…" I gave her a reassuring smile and patted the seat next to me.

"I just. Rose…you…I…" she paled and perched on the seat next to me. "I don't want you to get the wrong idea, it's just…You've become extremely important to me over the past couple of years and I don't want you to forget about me."

I nodded slowly and let her carry on talking.

"You know I didn't know anybody when I was signing up, I saw what seemed to be a friendly face and latched on and here we are. I consider you to be my best friend."

She paused and turned to face me. "I'm scared I'm going to lose you and I'm nowhere near as strong as you to deal with something like that, especially when it's somebody I care for so much."

I waved my hand to let her know I was about to say something and watched as she immediately bit her lip to stop talking.

"Why would I take that in the wrong way? I understand Betty. You're my best friend too and you know full well that when I'm back from Canada, the first person I will be seeing is you."

She nodded with a small smile and looked at the floor, "what if something happens to you on the boat? I've heard so many horror stories about crossings and I'd never find out!" She wailed so I wrapped my arms around my friend and rocked her until she had calmed enough to listen to reason.

"I will write a letter, if you get that letter then you know. But nothing is going to happen Betty, anyway why would I forget you? You're the person that took me in when I had nobody else in the world."

****

Chapter Fourteen

Getting ready for the boat journey was harder than I'd anticipated. They made sure that I was completely prepared for anything that could happen during the journey and taught me how to fire pretty much every gun I'd ever be able to lay my hands on. I'd like to have been able to say that it was all in vain but there were some very tense moments during the journey, especially when we sailed into the radar of an enemy submarine, the hour following the was spent in silence as we tried to silently maneuver around it without alerting the German's to our location.

This, however, didn't go to plan and I was quickly shoved away from the main deck so they could get everything sorted as quickly as possible. I was left standing in the kitchen with the chef, trying to ignore the sounds of whizzing torpedoes as they flew past the underside of the ship. The chef, a burly man with callous hands and greying hair, kept me entertained with his stories about his life and before I knew it we were back in safer waters. This wasn't the only time that it happened and by the time we were off the coast of Canada and were under threat yet again, I sort of wished that I had listened to Betty and stayed in London.

***

The first time I saw Edward was around a week after I'd arrived in Canada and even then it had only been a fleeting glance. I was expected to travel around a lot of the nurses' stations before I could go and look after my husband, so I actually did some work when I was out there. We chatted as much as we could when he came into the hospitals for check-ups, but it wasn't enough to placate me. By the time I was allowed to go to my husband, I was angry, upset and missing him more than anything.

"You're here!" he exclaimed when I finally walked out of the hospital after my last shift. I laughed sourly.

"I've been here for three weeks already." I snapped and leant my head against his chest.

"Well, you're here with me now, that's better than anything."

I sighed and looked up at him. His face was paler than it had been before; his eyes were very dark and looked as if he hadn't been getting much sleep. I gently laid my hands on his shoulder and frowned when I saw him try to contain his wince.

"Does it hurt?" I whispered as I lightly traced the sling that was holding his arm in place as it recovered from the surgery following the shooting.

He gritted his teeth and nodded shortly, "Only when you touch it." He hissed in pain, I gasped and immediately retracted my hands. He smiled softly and let out a long breath.

"Shall we get you back to mine then?"

I nodded and stooped down onto the floor to pick up my bag, my back cracked in the process and I whimpered.

"What was that?!" Edward asked and immediately came to my side, stretching out his one good hand to take my bag and help me stand up again.

"My back…it's because I've been bending over beds steadily for the past three weeks, it isn't used to it."

I tried to take the bag back from Edward, "Here, let me have it."

He shook his head and swung it over his shoulder, "I'm the gentleman here and I should carry your bag."

I bit my tongue and watched him walk off in front of me for a few paces.

"Edward!" I called out; he turned around and looked at me with a frown. "Edward, let me carry the bag."

He shook his head and defiantly walked off, though I could tell by the way he was ramrod straight that he was hurting. It didn't make any difference; there was nothing I could do that would change his mind and make him give me the bag.

***

I'd heard fleeting stories about Edward's life in Canada but nothing he said had warned me for the sheer size of his house.

"I thought you said you were…farmers…?" I wondered out loud, Edward laughed a little and nodded his head.

"We are…"

I looked at the building in front of me and then looked around bemused. "Where is the farm then?"

He laughed again and led me up to the door. It was a wooden house, which is what I'd been expecting, but it was larger than any farm I'd seen in England.

"Well, it's more a ranch now, the farm is out there." He pointed at a small piece of land in the far distance on his right.

"That's tiny!" I squeaked and walked into the house behind Edward, my breath caught in my throat. There were thick oak beams holding up the ceiling, which caused Edward to walk around the kitchen with his neck bent. When he took me into the living room, the ceiling became much higher and the room seemed more spacious.

"This used to be the stable." He explained with a small shrug and dropped my bag on to the floor beside a chair.

"My father loved to build things, so he spent most of the time extending the house when we moved."

I nodded and continued to look around in awe. There were net curtains hanging in front of several windows that adorned three out of four of the walls. The living room joined onto the dining room with a small step and wooden beams adorning either side of a small barrier.

"This is incredible." I muttered and reached out to touch one of the many frames on the walls.

Edward watched me with a smile on his face. "I suppose it is. It's much larger than our previous house."

"You moved?" I asked quickly and then blushed when I remembered that I'd already heard him tell me that. He laughed and nodded.

"We lived on the farm when I was younger."

I gasped and turned to face him, "How did you...move here?"

"My grandfather owned all of the land and had rented part of it to us when father lost his job. When my grandfather died, he left the rest of the land to us and we moved up here and used what little money we had to make my mother her dream home."

I smiled at him and wandered around the living room a little more, "Is there any more?" I asked sheepishly. Edward grinned at me and took my hand as he started to walk me around the rest of the house. What I thought had been the kitchen when I walked in was merely a meeting room at the front of the house. The kitchen was instead connected to the dining room on the opposite side to the living room and was massive. It had one of the largest AGA cookers I'd ever seen sat on the far wall, surrounded by cooking utensils I didn't even know the name of.

"My mother loves to cook so we made sure the kitchen was up to her standards. This was my father's greatest achievement; he had so much fun building it."

I ran my hand along the solid oak table in the centre of the room; there was an intricate design that had been drilled into the centre of it.

"That is my handiwork!" Edward beamed at me, "It took me three months, but I finally finished it."

I gasped, "That is amazing."

Edward laughed and let me out of the kitchen, "I have many hidden talents that you don't know about." He winked and chuckled as I blushed.

The tour of the rest of the house was over quite quickly after he'd shown me their inventive decision to enclose the bathroom at the back of the house so nobody had to walk miles to the outhouse. All that was left was his bedroom, his sister's room and the master bedroom.

When we made our way into his room, I gingerly sat down on the bed a breathed a sigh of amazement.

"I have never seen a house that looks like this before."

Edward sat next to me and winched as he knocked his shoulder on the back of the head board. I went to help him but he started to shake his head vigorously. "Don't, I'm fine." He hissed in pain and then puffed out short blasts of air as he worked through the agony.

***

At first, both of his parents were not entirely happy that I was there, taking up 'precious time' with their son. But after I'd been there for a couple of weeks, they seemed to let it go – though I was still sure they didn't really like me.

Edward spent a good few days trying to persuade me otherwise but it didn't matter because I was there to simply look after him. Not that he was going to let me.

"Sit still!" I hissed as I tried to peel the dressing on his wound away from his shoulder as gently as possible.

"I can do it myself!" He fought back.

"I'm the nurse here, this is the reason I'm here! Now sit still and stop complaining." I held my breath and concentrated on not knocking the healing scab. Edward jumped as the cold air hit the wound and twitched again.

"Edward Joseph McGraw! If you do not stay still then this is going to take longer to heal!"

"It hurts…" he whined and jerked away from my touch yet again.

"I know it does, but the quicker you let me do this, the quicker the pain will be over."

Sometimes it amazed me that Edward was a grown man, especially when it came to his shot wound. Every time I came anywhere near it, he would start wailing like a small child. It was cute at first, but after a while it just became annoying and I was getting increasingly aggravated with him.

"Edward! Will you please just stop moving, I'm supposed to be looking after you."

He narrowed his eyes at me and shook his head.

"I don't need looking after. I'm perfectly capable of cleaning this myself. I'd be much *gentler* anyway."

I pushed the cloth against his shoulder a little harder than necessary which caused him to hiss and cuss loudly. I tried to suppress my smirk.

"That hurt!"

I nodded, "It was supposed to. Now, sit still."

Once the kerfuffle of re-dressing his shoulder had passed; Edward calmed down instantly and stopped whining. Though, every time he wanted to do something that he'd been advised he couldn't, for instance re-decorating the living room, we started arguing again. He didn't seem to understand that he had to rest for everything to heal properly, otherwise he was going to make this worse and then it'd take longer for him to regain the use of his arm.

Although, when I told him this, he very fervently argued otherwise. Needless to say, anything involving his wound, the fact he was injured, or the fact I was there to help him ended up in arguments, ones that sometimes called for his parents to step in and split us up.

***

Once Edward had finally admitted defeat in relation to me nursing him, his injury started healing much faster. Within a month he had regained much more use of his arm and wasn't complaining when I had to change the gauze for him, though the fact he was better held other implications that I wasn't expecting.

It was a cloudy grey day in the middle of June, a rarity in Canada, when Edward walked into the house with a forlorn look on his face. I greeted him brightly from the kitchen and handed him a cup of tea I'd made when I heard the truck splutter up the long winding road.

"What's wrong?" I asked immediately, a sick feeling crept into my stomach. He gave me a forced smile and took the tea graciously.

"Nothing…" he paused to give me a kiss on the cheek and then walked into the living room, he sat down with a sigh.

"Edward, seriously, what is it?" I asked again as I watched his face anxiously. Something was wrong, something had happened and I wasn't going to let him get away with not telling me. He continued to shake his head.

"It's just something the doctor said. No need to worry your pretty little head about it." He gave me another forced smile and gazed out of the window. I hadn't realised that he had disappeared off to the doctors, in fact, he disappeared off quite a lot and I never knew where he seemed to go.

"Why didn't you tell me that you had a doctor's appointment?" I asked softly and perched on the edge of the chair. He looked up at me through tired eyes.

"Because I didn't think anything he had to say was going to be important."

I swallowed thickly, there were only two things – that I could think of – that the doctor had told him. Edward was either perfectly fine and the wound had healed like we'd hoped, or it had been infected and meant that there needed to be further operations.

"And was it…?" I slid onto the floor and knelt in front of him. I ignored the fact my skirt had bunched around my knees and was puffing out behind me, I ignored the fact that the wooden floor was scratching my legs and I ignored the fact that my clean apron was now being screwed up as I knelt, all I paid attention to was the fact that something was wrong with Edward and he wasn't going to let me in on it.

"Edward…"

He watched me with a sullen expression and rolled his eyes.

"The doctor said my shoulder was fine. It has healed better than they ever could have hoped for and although I will feel twinges from time to time, it's perfectly fine."

I jumped up with a massive grin and hugged him tightly. "Oh! That's wonderful! I'm so glad!" I laughed softly, "At least you know you can help your father in the living room when he starts up again."

He nodded slowly but the sullen look was still in place.

"Shouldn't you be extremely happy? This is what you wanted!"

I looked at him bemused and made myself comfortable on his lap before spouting off the things that we could get done now he could use his other arm.

"Rose..." I didn't hear him say my name so I just carried on talking.

"Then you could put up that picture frame your father can't reach!"

"Rose..." Although he spoke louder, I waved my hand around with a frown and carried on talking again, I was on a roll.

"Oh! And it means that we can finish the relay of the wood in the outdoor bathroom."

"Rose..."

I had a feeling that what he was going to say was going to be something that I didn't want to hear, so I spoke over him yet again and tried to ignore the look of anger that was crossing over his face.

"Then when it gets a bit warmer we can work on the cow pen and I can make you lemonade!"

"Rose!"

I clamped my mouth shut and turned to face him with wide eyes.

"Have you finished!?" he questioned exasperated. I nodded slowly and pursed my lips together to stop myself from rambling anymore.

"The doctor told me that everything was fine, but it comes at a price…"

He paused, ran a hand through his hair and swore quietly.

"I have to go back."

"Where?" I asked slowly, a sinking feeling crept into my stomach.

"The war, Rose. I have to go back and fight."

He stood up abruptly from the chair, knocking me over.

"I don't even have a week before I have to go back. He told my Captain the instance he'd finished with me."

I looked up at him with tears in my eyes and tried to get myself up off of the floor without breaking my composure.

"You have to go back to England."

"What?"

Edward sighed, "I'm not leaving you here. You're going back to England, Rose."

"What if I don't want to go back?" I cried in anguish. I'd grown quite accustomed to the lifestyle in Canada. It was quiet, stress free and much more liberating.

"Rose, you were here to look after me. I no longer need looking after, you have to go back."

I shook my head. "Is this simply because you don't want me here?"

Edward looked at me like I was stupid. "You think I don't want *you* here?"

I shrugged and walked over to the window. "I don't know Edward, you weren't happy when I was here to help you and now you're demanding that I go home!"

He walked up behind me, placed his hands on my shoulders and gave them a little squeeze.

"What on earth makes you think I don't want you here…?"

I turned to face him and raised an eyebrow. "We've argued more than I'd like to admit in the past month…"

Edward sighed and took one of his hands off of my shoulder to press it against my cheek.

"I wasn't arguing with you because I didn't want you to help me…"

I shrugged again and turned back to the window. "It doesn't matter. I'll leave as soon as I can."

He walked away from me and I heard his sigh from across the room. "Rooose!" He whined, I ignored him and watched the clouds in the sky.

"I felt invalid." He muttered and joined me at the window. "I hated that you had to look after me and I couldn't take care of you."

I glanced at him from the corner of my eyes and frowned. "You could do everything normally except move that arm…"

Edward sighed again. "That's not the point, it was still degrading. I couldn't clean myself properly and I had to rely on you."

I laughed bitterly, "Well, I'm sorry that I was such a burden."

He grabbed my arm and pulled me to face him. "Why are you being so difficult?"

"I'm not." I snapped and twisted out of his grasp. I watched his jaw tense as he shook his head in annoyance.

"I don't understand why you're so angry at me."

I frowned, "You don't understand why I'm angry?"

He shook his head. "No, I don't."

"Right, well let me put it this way. I've taken over two months out of my life in London to come over here and look after you."

I walked across to the other side of the living room and started to pace.

"I endured one of the scariest journeys of my life to then spend three weeks nursing other people before I could come here and be with you!"

He was watching me walk around with a stern look on his face.

"And here you are demanding that I return to London, telling me you felt invalid and in all honesty, you seem entirely ungrateful."

"I'm very grate-"

I put my hand up to quieten him. "Don't bother Edward; you've made it perfectly clear how you feel." I folded my arms across my chest and turned my back to him so I could walk to our room and start to get my stuff ready.

"Take me to the train station as soon as you think I should leave." I told him without so much as a backward glance.

****

Chapter Fifteen

Given that he had to start preparing to be shipped back off to war, I was taken to the train station the following morning. Any conversation between us had become strained and we spent the majority of our final hours together in silence. The goodbye at the train station was short and before I could really think about the way I was behaving, I'd already pulled out of the station and was on my way towards the port.

Edward had told me he loved me before I got on the train, but like the fool I was, I refused to say anything back since I was still upset. My childishness only ended up upsetting me more and I spent the entire train journey yearning for Edward so I could tell him that I loved him and that things were okay with us. On top of that, I hated that my last memory of him was with a heartbroken look on his face and tears in his eyes.

***

I had been hoping that the boat journey was going to be much smoother on the way back but I knew within minutes of leaving the port that things weren't going to be any easier. We were barely a mile away from the Canadian coast when the submarine siren started to wail, alerting us to a possible close by enemy. The Captain again threw me down into the kitchen with the chef but quickly changed his mind when he realised that we were going to be surrounded by enemy boats within a couple of minutes. He threw open the kitchen door and looked around frantically.

"Where is she?" He yelled at the chef before I was spotted in the corner of the room.

"You!" He pointed a chubby finger at me and beckoned me over. I had to bite back a laugh at the look on his face. It was quickly becoming a purple like red and was rather comical when paired with his wispy moustache that seemed to have a mind of its own.

"Yes, Sir?" I quickly made my way around the kitchen counters and stood next to him.

"Have you got something a little more…practical to wear?" He questioned whilst motioning to the dress I was wearing. I glanced down and ran my hands across the side of the skirt in nervousness.

"No Sir…"

He growled and turned on his heel. "I want you on the deck in no more than five minutes. I'll get one of my men to give you something to wear, I'm sure somebody will have clothes that will…fit."

"Sir? What's going on?"

He looked over his shoulder at me and raised an eyebrow. "We're about to be attacked and need as much power as we can have. I was assured that you had the training." He narrowed his eyes as he spat out his words.

I nodded quickly, "Yes of course I did, Sir."

"Good, now get up to the deck as quickly as you can."

He stormed out of the room and slammed the door shut behind him. I cast a nervous glance over at the chef who was watching me with wide eyes. "Good luck…" he muttered with a pale face.

I nodded and pulled out the letter addressed to Betty that I had kept on me at all times.

"If something…*bad* were to happen to me, could you make sure this reaches the recipient please?" I asked quickly as I shoved the letter at him, "Please, it's important."

***

As soon as I made my way onto the deck, I was quickly carted off to a guy that had a spare set of more 'appropriate' clothing for me. By the time I was ready to get involved in whatever it was that they wanted me to do, a very serious tone had been taken on board. In this distance there were several black looming ships that seemed to be increasing their speed towards us and by the sound of the siren that was still wailing there were several submarines close by.

"Captain, what is going on?" I asked him seconds before the ship was knocked to the side by a brutal force and started to shake.

He handed me a heavy strip of ammo and pushed me towards one of the many machine guns that adorned the side of the boat.

"Shoot now, ask questions later."

I watched the people around me with wide eyes and tried to figure out what the hell was going on.

"How are the guns going to compare against torpedoes?" I asked quietly and winced when I saw the look on the Captain's face.

"Shoot now, questions later…" I repeated and ran the length of the ship, dodging pieces of debris that started to fly towards us as the other ships opened fire. One of the sailors grabbed me and threw me behind a pile of sandbags.

"Stay. There." He hissed and snatched the ammo from me. I went to protest but he'd already turned his attention back to loading the gun in front of him.

"Bloody hell," he cursed as a bullet whizzed past his ear and lodged itself into the wooden pole behind him. I curled in on myself even more and made sure that I was completely surrounded by the bags.

"What's going on?" I yelled above the drone of the machine gun fire. There were a few tense moments when the sailor didn't answer me and I wondered briefly if he'd been shot, but he peeked his head over the top of one of the sandbags and looked at me.

"We are in the middle of a trap that the German's have set. Now stay there, I don't want your death on my hands." He threw himself flat on the ground as another series of bullets shot past and hit one of the top sandbags. I cowered even further on the floor and covered my head.

"You all right?" The sailor called, I squeaked in answer and started to pray that we would get out of this alive.

"Do you need any help?" I shouted and peered over the top of my little hiding place. The ships that had been in the distance when I'd first noticed them were surrounding us and another of our fleet completely. The side of our ship was stained with bullet holes and there was a lot of blood splattered around the place. The sailor I was talking to immediately turned around to face me.

"No! What did I say? Get back down ther-"

I heard a thud before the centre of his shirt was stained a very dark red and blood started to bubble at his mouth. With wide eyes he looked down at his abdomen before looking at me again. I started to scream but that was quickly cut off as another bullet hit square in the back of the head. I opened my mouth to scream again but instead found that I violently emptied the contents of my stomach. As I continued retching, I heard the screams from the sailors quieten as they realised what had just happened.

"Shit! Kenneth has been shot!" Another sailor cried as he ran over to the gun and swiftly grabbed his colleague's legs so he could move the body away from it.

"You! There!" He pointed at me and then at the gun. "You get those bastards back for killing one of our best." He hissed and dragged the remnants of his friend across the ship deck, dodging the sprays of ammo that were relentlessly aimed at us. I stayed hidden for a few more moments trying to think of the best way to get out of shooting but the Captain had kept a close eye on me and was not having any of it.

"Get on that gun this instant young lady or I will throw you to the Jerrys!" He screamed at me and grabbed at my arm. Although I would have normally begged to be let go and then would have hidden somewhere else, I swallowed my fear and lurched myself at the gun, hiding behind its protective shield merely seconds before another round of bullets came flying in our direction.

"You best bloody kill some of these guys duck, or I ain't going to be pleased. You're the reason Ken died."

I ignored the Captain and turned my attention to a series of three gunmen standing of the ship opposite. It appeared that they didn't realise there was somebody currently manning my gun, so I took the opportunity to shoot and hoped that I hit something that wasn't one of our own. I squeezed the trigger with trepidation and watched in amazement as each bullet hit its target. Two of three men fell to the floor in a bloody heap and the last man quickly turned to face my direction in fear and confusion. His hand closed over the trigger at the same time I flexed my fingers again, he fell down with a satisfying scream and a thud.

With a somewhat maniacal laugh, I pressed down the trigger yet again and watched happily as man after man fell in a heap. They didn't expect to see me, they didn't know I was there and from my vantage point I could see every move that they were making. I kept each burst of ammo short so they couldn't figure out which direction it was all coming from and made sure that no part of my body was visible above the side of the ship.

It was much easier for me to hide than it was for the burly sailors since I was much smaller and I kept giggling to myself as I watched the others try and copy my actions, they could barely hide from the edge of the ship, let alone curl up underneath the gun.

The Captain kept shooting me looks of shock and awe when he saw that I was mindlessly killing men whenever I saw them on the opposing ships. I was a little surprised myself, I thought I would've cared a little more about the fact that I was destroying the lives of men that I'd never met, but given everything that had happened to me over the past four years, I felt empowered. I was finally getting the revenge I'd been yearning for and it was fun.

"Oi, lassy! Perhaps lay off the gun for a while." One sailor called from behind me.

"Yeah! Leave some bastards for us!" Another shouted from the deck. Just to annoy the both of them, I swung the gun around and pointed it at a different ship before letting all hell break loose.

The noise of glee that escaped my lips when I saw another several men drop was like nothing I'd ever heard before, nor was it like any other noise I'd ever made. I was beginning to scare myself but it didn't make me slow down my killing spree any more. I was shaken out of my mania briefly when the ship was hit below the bow again and sent everybody flying. I shot a look over to the Captain, who quickly jerked his head in the direction of the torpedo unit. I scurried past him with my head down and saluted swiftly as I made my way down into the heart of the ship.

I could hear the shouts of men that were struggling in a room that was quickly flooding, yet instead of stopping to help them, I carried on to my destination. When I opened the door to what I had nicknamed the 'torpedo centre', the entire group of men in there looked at me like I was insane.

"What the hell do you think you're doing in here?" One shouted.

"Get the hell out of here!" Another called.

"Why is a *girl* on the boat?!" A third questioned.

"Captain sent me."

The eldest of the men walked over and peered at me over the top of his thick rimmed glasses. He raised a sandy eyebrow and shook his mane of hair.

"And we're supposed to believe that?" He snorted and clicked his tongue against his teeth.

"Get out of here before you get yourself hurt!" He hissed and pushed me towards the door. I planted my feet on the ground and fought as hard as I could so I didn't get moved.

"This is no place for a young girl. Go back to wherever you were hiding. I'm sure the Captain wouldn't be pleased to know we have a stowaway."

I shook my head and pried his fingers off of my arm.

"I told you already, the Captain sent me."

"Why on bloody earth would the Captain send *you* down here?"

I rolled my eyes and tutted. "Maybe it's because he thought you lot needed a change of scenery..." I fluttered my eyelashes and then folded my arms across my chest and raised an eyebrow. "Or, maybe it's because I just killed 40 guys in 10 minutes."

A hush fell across the room, "Now, if you don't mind, could you please show me to the torpedo shooter? I'm on a roll here and I don't want to stop because some *ignorant* male doesn't think a woman should be down here. Furthermore, I'm sure the Captain would love to know just how much work you *really* are doing here."

I was quickly taken to where I needed to be and then left to my own devices. I had never once spoken to anybody like that before and wasn't really planning on making a habit of it, but desperate times called for desperate measures.

***

I wasn't able to see the level of my destruction very well when operating the torpedoes and it put a slight dampener on my mood, though every time I heard a loud crunching explosion I knew I'd made contact and that was just as exciting.

"Where the hell did you get your training?" The eldest man walked over to me again and watched in awe as I struck my target head on,

"I mean, I have some of the best men on my team and, dare I say it, you're verging on being better than them."

I snorted, "I pick things up quickly."

"No kidding."

"I was trained in London anyway. They weren't sure if the crossing to Canada was going to be safe enough for me to be untrained so they ran me through things."

The guy nodded and turned back to his men.

"Just keep an eye on this one. She seems like a loose cannon."

I went to shout at him, or say something to fight back but then he turned to face me and gave me a little wink. "That'll get them working better, give them a little competition."

***

It took hours but finally, after the help of another fleet of ships, we managed to destroy the Germans that had surrounded us. I was congratulated about my skills and the amount of people I'd shot before everybody returned back to their original posts and continued the journey like nothing had happened.

By the time I arrived back to England, there was a kind of entourage that met me. Betty was at the front with a massive smile on her face. I ran over to her and gave her a massive hug before I bid farewell to the men I'd travelled with and breathed a sigh of relief that I'd made it home safely.

"We heard about the German fleet..." she whispered on the train when we'd managed to make our way into a relevantly empty carriage.

"How?"

"The communicator on the ship contacted us as soon as you were called up to help. He wanted us to know if anything happened."

I nodded and shuddered with the chill of the air.

"I cannot believe you did that!" she hissed. I wasn't sure if she was excited or annoyed.

"You could have gotten yourself killed."

I sighed and leant back against the chair. "I'm fine, though I did end up getting one of the sailor's killed."

Betty paled and buried her head in her hands. "Dare I ask how you managed that?"

I gave a little laugh, "I asked him if he needed help, he stood up to tell me he was fine and to stay quiet when he was shot in the back and then in the head."

"He was shot in front of you?" she cried. I nodded slowly and swallowed down the bile that was quickly rising in my throat.

"How did you..." she paused and rubbed the back of her neck. "How did you cope?"

"Got the revenge I've been wanting for ages."

Betty nodded and closed her eyes slowly. "I want to hear about that, but not right now. I'm just glad you're safe."

She turned her attention out of the window and watched as the world passed her by. I glanced over but didn't focus on anything; instead I was just happy to be back on solid ground for the first time in a while.

"How was Edward?" she asked a little bit later. I gave a short laugh.

"He's better, he's been sent back out to fight."

Betty gasped, "Really? Is that why you came back?"

I nodded slowly, "he told me I needed to come back and then we got into a massive argument. I left the next day."

She frowned, "Oh, what are you going to do now?"

I shrugged "I don't know we didn't sort anything out. I guess I'll just have to wait and see when the war is over."

Betty hummed in agreement.

"But I don't think I'll go back to Canada for a while – too much blood for me." I smiled at Betty and then closed my eyes again.

＊＊＊＊

Chapter Sixteen

Present Day

"Wait. What?" Trent quickly interrupted me, his face a picture of concern. "Repeat what just happened…"

"I was on the train with Betty on the way back to London and -"

"No, Nanna. The part beforehand."

I giggled a little, the look of concern and ultimately confusion on his face was a picture.

"I saw a man get shot in front of me…?" I offered with a small smile. He shook his head vigorously.

"You never told us you killed people." Elsie clarified. "I've heard this story 20 different times and you never told me you shot people…"

I shrugged and wriggled about on the bed until I was comfortable yet again. "I didn't think it was that important."

There was a pause as everybody in the room fell silent. "How many did you kill…?" Trent asked slowly. I furrowed my eyebrows in thought.

"I…erm…I don't remember."

"You don't remember or you don't want to tell us?" He questioned tightly.

"It was more than about 50; if that's any help."

He sighed and shook his head in disgust.

"That's so…"

"Cool!" Suzie piped up and looked at me with excited eyes. "I can't believe you did that! That's incredible!"

I breathed a sigh of relief as everybody's attention quickly turned to her.

"Suzie…how could you say that?" Isaac, my second eldest grandson, spoke for the first time since he entered the room. He flicked his gaze towards me and bit his lip in thought.

"Because she wanted to get her revenge!" She turned to face her brother and shook her head. "I don't understand why that's such a bad thing. I mean, if she did it now then okay fair enough be disgusted."

Suzie quickly leant over the bed and kissed me on the cheek, "but given the state of the world at the time and it was a matter of life and death, then I think it's incredible."

I gave her a warm smile, "thank you, darling."

"I still think it's disgusting. Think about the families of those you killed."

I narrowed my eyes at Isaac and sighed. "Things at this time are completely different to how they were back then. You can't say you think something is disgusting since you weren't alive then."

"Yes but even if I was alive back then, I wouldn't have done anything like that. You effectively murdered all those people."

I bit my lip as I tried to think of something to say that didn't end up coming across snappy.

"Did they care when they killed my family? When they hurt everybody I loved? No. That didn't cross their minds, so why should it have been different for me." I took a deep breath and closed my eyes for a split second, trying to calm down. "It was either kill or be killed. If I didn't kill those people then I would've been killed myself and *none* of you would be here right now!"

Isaac opened his mouth to say something and then immediately shut it, a move that he did a couple of times. Suzie winked and me and shoved her brother in the arm.

"Apologise to Nanna!"

Isaac rolled his eyes and stuck his tongue out at his younger sister. "Sorry Nanna."

I laughed and gave him a smile. "Right, well. Can I get on with my story now?"

"Is there any more killing?" Trent asked me quickly with a weird look on his face.

"No, no more killing."

"Then you're more than welcome to go ahead."

****

Chapter Seventeen
1943

"Rose, will you please get out of bed and open the letters on the table for you?" Betty banged on my bedroom door for the third time. I buried my head under the pillow and chose to ignore her, again.

"Seriously, I want to know what they are! They look really official!"

I groaned and yelled back at her. "If you're that bothered open them yourself. It doesn't matter to me either way." I couldn't help but smile as I heard the squeal of delight before I heard her feet padding away from the door. I had just managed to drift back off to sleep when a piercing scream broke the silence in the house.

"Rose!" Betty screeched and threw open my door, not caring that it slammed into my dresser and knocked several things over. I groaned as I heard them clang together on the floor.

"What is it Betty?" I tried to look interested but the chances of it being something that really mattered were quite slim, she over-reacted a lot.

"You know those letters that were addressed to you on the table?" she chirped and started waving several pieces of paper around in my face before she jumped onto the bed and lay down next to me.

"Yes…"

"Well I was right, they were very official!" She grinned at me. "Extremely official. So official that you will be meeting the Prime Minister…"

I raised an eyebrow, "Really? Why?"

She moved the letters out of my reach and then giggled like a small child. "Well I don't know if I should tell you, after all you did say it didn't matter."

I sighed in annoyance. "Betty, give me the letters."

She shook her head and bounded off of the bed. "You'll have to come and get them."

"What are we? Five? Betty, just give them to me."

I jumped out of the bed and walked towards her. Once I neared my dresser I realised that my jewellery box was in a heap on the floor and narrowed my eyes at Betty. "You've made a mess of my room Betty, the least you could do is give me the letter."

She shook her head again and ran out of the room grinning wildly at me as she waited for me to chase her. I didn't, I just very patiently waited until she got bored hiding the paper from me and snatched it from her when she least expected it. It wasn't the wisest of ideas as the instance my back was turned she tackled me to the floor and pinned my hands either side of my body.

"That's unfair!" she wailed and tried to grab the letter from my fist. I sighed and wriggled around until she lost her balance so I could roll over on to my stomach, allowing me to read it without her trying to get it back. She fell to the side and started to sulk.

"This wouldn't have happened if you just gave me the bloody letters in the first place!"

Betty huffed and put her arms around her legs. I scanned the letter quickly to figure out what she had been talking about and barely suppressed my own scream when I read the opening sentence of the middle paragraph.

We would like to award you with the Royal Red Cross, Mrs McGraw, for the exceptional work you have been doing all over the country.

I glanced over at Betty who was intently watching me. "Is this for real?"

She nodded quickly, "I told you it looked official."

I raised one side of my mouth in a half smile and turned back to the letter.

In light of your recent bravery during a journey back from Canada, we would also like to award you with the George Cross.

Mrs McGraw, we are humbled by the way you have faced danger in the last five years and would like to celebrate this alongside you.

"Two!?" I squeaked, Betty came to lie down beside me and continued to nod her head.

"I don't think I know of anybody else who has been awarded two…"

I read the letter for a second time, in case I had misread something and that it wasn't telling me what I thought it was.

"I don't understand…" I mumbled and got up off of the floor before quickly falling into one of the chairs. "I don't understand how they'd know…"

Betty followed suit and sat in the chair opposite me. "Well, you remember how I told you that the communications person had gotten into contact with us the instance you were asked to help?"

I nodded slowly, "Yeah…"

"Well, they let us know after it had all calmed down what happened."

"Right…"

Betty's face broke out into a grin. "I passed the information on to the relevant people."

I shot my eyes up to her face. "*You* did this?"

She nodded, "Well. I was the one that told them about it all…"

"Why…?"

"Because you're incredible."

I shook my head, "Anybody would have done the same thing if they were in the same situation as me!"

She shrugged, "That may be the case, but I thought it was worth celebrating."

***

I wrote an answering letter to the Prime Minister's secretary as soon as I could and was informed that even though they were very impressed with my actions, they would not be having any ceremony until it was safer for England. They, sneakily, told me that the threat of invasion was still rife and it would be until they caught Hitler. They also assured me that it was only a matter of time until this happened but it was still going to take some time to find him.

I was a little shocked at how bluntly they informed me with what was going on, especially since the government had relentlessly reminded us that 'careless talk costs lives' but I pretended not to be shocked and promised profusely that I would not repeat the information to anybody else. A promise that I found incredibly hard to keep when Betty started interrogating me, wanting to know exactly what they had told me and when the ceremony would happen. Somehow, I managed to steer her away from wanting to know all the details of the conversations but it was not particularly easy.

***

One day after we'd arrived back at the flat after patrolling, Betty immediately dragged me into my room and started to go through my closet, looking for something 'suitable' that I could wear. I didn't question her motives until she pulled out a dress that I had been given by Edward's mother when I was in Canada.

"What…are you doing?" I asked slowly, she turned to face me with a bright smile.

"Well, I thought we could go out and celebrate your amazing achievement…"

I narrowed my eyes, she knew I wasn't entirely comfortable with social events, I'd told her what had happened at the Christmas dance in 1939 several times.

"Where…?"

She laid the dress on the bed and skipped over to my dresser before yanking open my jewellery box and shifting through my small selection of necklaces. "Well, there's this pub in East London that Pat said was quite nice."

I groaned and shook my head, "Betty, I'm not in any way going to enjoy going out."

She picked up a necklace that my mother had given me for my 18th birthday, a small silver necklace with a rose pendent, and laid it on top of the dress.

"I'm not taking no for an answer, we're going out. We don't even have to stay out later than 9 Rose!"

I sighed, "Betty, this really isn't my-"

She interrupted me with a wave of her hand. "Pat hasn't seen you since you buggered off to Canada, either you come out with us tonight or he'll hunt you down and force you out later."

152

I went to open my mouth to argue again but she continued talking over me.

"We've all had a horrendous few years and it's time just to relax and have fun."

"But-"

"You're going Rose and that's that." Betty didn't even wait for me to answer; she walked out of the room and slammed the door behind her before very quickly calling out, "Be ready in an hour."

***

I complained about her idea of going out the entire time we made our way across London. I continued to complain as we met up with friends and had to force a smile when people came up to congratulate me about my medals. I was still complaining by the time Pat turned up and that was a few hours after us.

"What's her problem?" I heard Pat ask Betty when I was otherwise engaged with a group of people from the Ambulance Dispatch.

"She didn't want to come out tonight..."

"Did you tell her what it was for?" He asked with a sideways glance at me. I quickly pretended I was in a deep conversation with the person stood in front of me.

"I told her it was so we could relax..." Betty shrugged, "I didn't know what else to say!"

"Why did you not just tell her that it was *for* her?" Pat hissed. I turned around open-mouthed.

"Because, I was leaving that up to you!" Betty looked at the shock on my face and then giggled. "And by the looks of things, you just told her."

I stared at them with a frown for a few seconds before I could even begin to think of how to ask them what was going on.

"Wh..." I rubbed my forehead. "What's going on?"

Pat sighed, pulled me to his side and took me to the bar.

"What are you drinking?" he asked quickly as the bartender made her way over to us. He sighed again as I didn't answer and ordered us two whiskey's.

"Something is telling me you'll need a strong drink to get through tonight."

"What is tonight?"

Pat scratched the back of his neck and looked at me sheepishly. "Well, Betty was somewhat right by saying it was to relax…"

"But…?"

"But…but it's mainly for you. To celebrate you."

I stared at him with wide eyes, "Why are you celebrating me?"

Pat grabbed the drinks off the side and downed them in succession, I eyed him in amusement. He drew the back of his hand across his mouth and turned to face me with another sheepish smile.

"When was the last time you celebrated your birthday?"

I opened my mouth to speak but struggled to think of the answer. "I think I was 19…so 1940."

Pat nodded and leant against the bar, motioning to the stool so I could sit down.

"That was years ago duck. You're 22 now, did you realise that?"

I gasped, it had been 3 years since I'd last remembered it was my birthday?

"I'll take that gasp as a no then…" He handed me my drink and perched on the stool behind him. I smiled gratefully and quickly demolished it. He was right; I was going to need a strong drink.

"You were married 2 years ago…" He mentioned, I shook my head slowly. That couldn't be right.

"Rose, let me ask you something…"

I nodded to let him know he could carry on.

"What year do you think it is?"

I paled when I tried to remember and realised that I couldn't.

"I...I don't know...?"

Pat smiled softly and put his arm around my shoulders. "You see, this is why we're celebrating you."

I frowned, "You're celebrating me because I can't remember the year?"

He laughed and squeezed me tighter. "No, though I suppose that is part of the reason why we're here."

I blinked a couple of times as I tried to figure out what he meant.

"I'm sorry, I don't follow you..."

He laughed again, "You have been amazing over the past few years, to the point that you don't remember what year it is." He paused, handed me another drink and then started walking back to the rest of the group, I jumped off of the stool and followed him.

"You've been working so hard that you bypassed your birthdays and anniversaries without a backwards glance."

He turned to face me and held onto one of my shoulders with a squeeze. "You're an inspiration to all of us because you lost your family, nearly lost your husband and here you are, four years later, still fighting for what is right."

I shrugged, "Anybody would've done it..."

"I wouldn't! I don't think I could have coped if I lost my family and my life..."

I shook my head, "It isn't something to celebrate. It was the only thing I could do."

Pat dropped his drink onto the table and turned back to me with a determined look on his face.

"You don't understand it do you?" he paused and grabbed both of my arms. "Rose, we're so proud of you. More than you'll ever know. We've seen people throw themselves into the Thames because they couldn't handle life anymore and they had to handle things much easier than you, yet you're still here!"

"I -" He held up his hand to stop me talking and carried on.

"You went over to Canada to look after your husband when it really wasn't safe. You didn't run scared in the face of danger on the way back; you were up there with the best of them as you fought against evil. You've been awarded two medals for your work during this bloody war! You're so much stronger now, mentally and emotionally, than you were when I first met you. You've grown so much over the past 4 years and it's the least we could do."

I chose not to argue when I noticed that he was beginning to cry.

"If I could be half the person that you are Rose, I'd be extremely honoured. And believe me when I say that Edward is a lucky, lucky man."

I bit my lip to try and fight back my own tears and wrapped my arms around his neck. "Thank you."

He leant back, kissed my forehead and gave me a watery grin.

"Now that's out of the way, can we please enjoy ourselves?"

***

After the tense moments at the beginning of the night, I finally calmed down enough to enjoy my time out. Although I still felt a little uneasy about the fact that everybody was there to celebrate *me*, I stopped complaining about it. There was one thing however that was still bothering me slightly I made sure to ask Betty when she flitted over with a massive smile and a slightly tipsy giggle.

"There you are stranger!" she smiled widely at me and sat down next to me on the seat. "Where have you been hiding?"

I gave her a small smile and bumped her shoulder with mine, causing her to sway dramatically. We both giggled.

"I've not been hiding!"

Betty snorted and took another mouthful of her drink. "I haven't seen you for the past half an hour!"

I laughed and eyed the guy she'd been talking to at the bar.

"Well, I believe it's due to the fact you were rather occupied with the chap at the bar."

She blushed and ducked her head. "We were only talking…"

"I could see that…"

She swatted me on the arm and pouted.

"Betty, what year is it?"

She choked on the liquid she had in her mouth. "Sorry?"

"What year is it?" I repeated and gave her a shy smile.

"Why do you want to know what the year is?" She questioned slowly and turned to face me completely, a frown etched out on her face.

"Because…" I sighed, "Because I don't remember what year it is…" I admitted nervously. She gasped and patted my arm.

"It's 1943…"

"Oh…"

Betty giggled a little, "Do you need another drink?"

"Yeah…" I wailed and buried my head in my hands, shaking it repeatedly. "In fact, just get me the entire bottle of whiskey."

Betty snorted before running up to the bar and returning with the bottle. "As long as you share it, you can have it."

I nodded emphatically and snatched the bottle from her hand, before wincing and coughing as the liquid burnt my throat.

***

Perhaps getting a bottle of whiskey hadn't been the wisest of decisions and I was aware that I was going to regret it in the morning, but at that moment, I couldn't bring myself to care.

"Roooooooooose!" Betty squealed from the opposite side of the room. "The bottle is empty!" She pouted and turned it upside down, watching forlornly as the last few drops dripped onto the floor.

"Waste not, want not." She chirped before dropping to her knees and sticking her tongue out. She came dangerously close to licking the floor but I grabbed her hair just before she could connect. Pat was sat at the bar shaking his head at the both of us.

"You two are incredible." He muttered angrily though I could tell he was trying to suppress a smile. He picked Betty up by her armpits and plonked the squealing girl onto the stool he had just vacated.

"Maybe some water would be a good idea for you two." He stated rather than asked.

"I don't need any! I'm not drunk!" I hiccupped but covered it with a little cough before smiling brilliantly at Pat. "See, I can walk perfectly fine."

I frowned in concentration as I made the short journey to the bar. Everything had been going incredibly well until I stumbled on something on the floor and fell into the corner of the table.

"That's not fair! I was tripped!" I squealed when Pat picked me up and sat me next to Betty, I turned to narrow my eyes at the part of the floor I had tripped on.

"Over air Rose, you tripped over air…" He handed us both two big glasses of water and waited patiently until we'd finished it.

"Now, do I have to walk you two girls home or will you be all right?"

I jumped off of the stool and grabbed Betty's arm. She was sat there giggling to herself about something or another.

"I'll be perfectly fine walking how. I'm *not* drunk." I raised a pointed finger at him and poked him on the nose. Pat rolled his eyes and thrust another glass of water in my hand.

"That's a matter of opinion... "

I narrowed my eyes at him and placed the glass on the bar before winding my arm around Betty's waist and dragging her off of the stool. She squealed in delight again and started to giggle more.

"You have a pretty face!" she declared whilst wiggling in my arms until she made sure we were standing face to face. "It's really nice..."

I laughed and stepped back so there was a little space between us, mainly so I was able to hold the both of us up if she started to sway any more.

"Thanks...?" I laughed and maneuvered her around until she was sat down on one of the more comfortable seats. I was about to walk away and find her coat for her when she grabbed my arm and pulled me into her lap.

"Edward is a lucky man." She hiccupped and grinned toothily at me. "But he doesn't know how lucky he is..."

I raised an eyebrow and tried to get out of her grip. "Where are you going?" She stuck out her bottom lip in a pout and looked at me through her eyelashes. I laughed, moved a strand of hair out of her face and tried to stand up again.

"I think it's time we headed home Betty. I was just getting your coat."

Her arms tightened around my waist. For such a small lady, she was surprisingly strong.

"No... don't want to leave." She grumbled and buried her head into the back of my neck. Her short breaths started to tickle me.

"Betty! Let me go!" I squealed and when she caught on to what was making me laugh, she made it worse before tickling my sides. I shrieked.

"What are you doing!?" I couldn't breathe because I was laughing so much.

She feigned innocence, "Who? Me...? Nothing!"

I rolled my eyes and struggled once again to get out of her grip. I blamed the alcohol intake for the fact that I was yet again unable to break free.

"You're not going anywhere." She chirped. I laughed in agreement.

"It appears that I'm not..."

She winked, "Which is how I planned it."

I studied her face from over my shoulder and frowned when I noticed the weird look she was wearing. There seemed to be a shift in the mood surrounding us.

"You really are pretty..."

I blushed and shook my head; I didn't really know what I could say.

"Betty, I think it's time that we made our way home..." I hissed and pried her hands off of my waist. "We've both had enough to drink." I gave her smile and held out my hand. She looked sad for a couple of seconds before she took my hand and jumped up. I steadied her as she stumbled and grabbed both of our coats.

"Finally admitted defeat?" Pat mused as he watched me struggle to walk with Betty attached to my hip. I nodded and kissed him on the cheek in goodbye.

"I'm not the drunk one, as you can see!" I called over my shoulder when I turned to leave. He laughed.

"Well, we'll see in the morning!" He winked and waved. "Safe journey!"

I stumbled out of the door with Betty in tow. The brisk evening air hit us full force and we stopped momentarily to button up our coats before carrying on the arduous journey.

****

Chapter Eighteen

It was quite quiet on the Home Front during the period between 1943 and 1945. Life pretty much stayed the same, there were no bombs being dropped on London and we all fell into this false sense of security. Nobody knew what the next move was going to be by Hitler but we had a feeling that he was beginning to struggle. No information of major importance had been leaked but there was an overall feeling that we had started to win the war. We just hoped that this turned out to be true.

Due to the extensive time Edward had taken off, away from his duties, he wasn't allowed to take any more leave from the army. The reason, he'd told me, was that they found him too invaluable and couldn't deal without him there. Although part of me believed him, I was a little worried that it had something to do with him not wanting to see me after the way things had been left in Canada. Yet, when I'd mentioned this, he'd apologised to me immediately and told me that he wasn't upset with me but rather he was upset with himself and had been harbouring the annoyance since I left. I had tried apologising since I was partly to blame for the iciness of the situation, but he wouldn't accept it or any version of an apology that I tried to give.

Although we tried extremely hard to keep in contact with each other as often as possible, the letters being sent between Edward and I became very far and very few between until I received the final one at the beginning of 1945.

Rose,

I love you. I love you more than anything, but I cannot write to you anymore. Things are getting too – dangerous. I need to keep my wits about me. I will explain all when I am with you next. I am sorry that this letter is so short, but I am running out of time.

I'll see you soon my love.

Edward.

The day I read it, I broke down in a heap on the floor. Betty wasn't home at the time, but she reappeared a couple of hours later and found me in exactly the same position. At first she didn't understand what was going on, but as soon as I showed her the letter, she was on the floor next to me, comforting me.

"Ssssh." She cooed as I started crying again.

"What if something happens and I don't find out?" I wailed and buried my head in my hands. I started to rock in despair. "What if something really bad happens and I don't get to know?"

Betty sighed and started to stroke the back of my hair. "They told you before that he was shot, didn't they?"

I nodded slowly, "Yeah…I suppose they did."

Betty gave me a small smile. "Then what's stopping them from telling you if something else happens?"

I whimpered, "But what if it's too dangerous and they can't let me know?"

I managed to pull myself up off of the floor and looked at Betty with wide eyes. If it was too dangerous for him to contact me it would surely be too dangerous for any officials.

"Rose, I'm sure you have nothing to worry about." Betty shrugged, "And if anything was to happen, they'd find a way for you to find out. They have to."

***

I didn't hold much hope for 1945. I was pretty sure that it was going to be the same as the previous four years and that would mean that it was going to be difficult and very painful to deal with. What made things worse was the lack of contact that I had with Edward. Even though it was the beginning of the year, it was already taking its toll on me and I hated to think of how affected by it I would be later on.

***

It was becoming entirely too common an occurrence for me to be woken up by Betty screeching at my door. May the 7th wasn't any different.

"Rose!" I heard the banging of my door in my dream before her voice floated through. I scrunched my eyes up tighter and groaned. She was too excitable.

"Rose!" she barged in, let the door hit my dress table – again – and jumped onto the bed. I quickly buried my head under the pillow and clamped my arms over the top of it. I really didn't want to know what she had to say.

"Rose, c'mon! It's important!"

"Ismttvalwiz." I retorted underneath the pillow.

She giggled and pulled the pillow off of my head. "I'd understand you better if you spoke English…or you know, didn't speak into the pillow." She smiled at me.

I sighed and repeated myself, "I said, isn't it always?"

For a split second a hurt look passed over Betty's face, but as soon as I'd noticed it, it was gone again. She gave me another brilliant smile.

"Well this time it really is important."

I nodded and waited for her to carry on explaining. I felt a little bad for upsetting her when I hadn't intended to.

"What's the date today?" Betty asked quickly, I frowned and shrugged.

"Um…May 7th? How is this relevant?" I snapped. Betty patted my knee and continued to grin despite my rudeness.

"Tomorrow is May 8th then, right?"

I nodded slowly, "That is what usually follows the 7th…yes…"

"Well, I just heard on the radio that…" she paused for suspense. I bit my tongue to stop from saying anything else hurtful.

"May 8th will be Victory in Europe day…!"

I stared at her blankly for a few minutes.

"Sorry? What was that?" I questioned quietly. She couldn't have said what I'd thought she'd said. If she had, it was something that we'd all been waiting for, for years.

"Tomorrow will be Victory in Europe day."

I continued to stare at her blankly.

"Tomorrow the war will have ended!" Betty clarified and then squealed.

"Everything will be over! Everybody will start coming home!"

I shook my head in disbelief. "You can't be serious, it can't have ended."

Betty laughed and wrapped her arms around me in a quick joyful hug. "It was just broadcast by the BBC on the radio. It's real darling."

***

I spent much of the day in a haze. The war was going to be over in a matter of hours and then they'd start sending everybody home to their families. We'd finally survived everything, we'd survived the bombings, the destruction, the loss and we'd lived to tell the tale.

Part of me was ecstatic that it was going to be over, that everything was going to slowly return to normal but there was a part of me that felt insanely guilty. I felt guilty because the majority of my family weren't going to able to celebrate the ending of the war, the ending of something that destroyed all our lives and because I'd complained I was bored, many years ago, I'd survived.

***

By the time the next morning came around I was a nervous mess. I was terrified that something had gone wrong and the war hadn't actually ended, instead they had actually found something else to fight about. I barely slept and was awake before Betty, which very rarely happened. She walked out of her room bleary eyed and stared at me in shock.

"Are you feeling okay?" she asked as she squeezed past me and moved around in the kitchen to make herself a cup of tea. I nodded and continued to bounce my leg in anxiety. I had been waiting by the radio for hours in case an emergency broadcast was called early in the morning. Nothing so far had happened.

"You look like hell…" she muttered and squeezed back past me so she could sit on the chair opposite.

"Thank you."

"I didn't mean it like that!"

I snorted and shook my head, bringing my already cold tea up to my mouth. It was the third cup I'd wasted. I put the cup back on the table and sighed.

"What's wrong?" Betty asked slowly after she'd woken up a little more.

"I'm just scared…" I shrugged and fiddled around with the dials on the wireless. I had somehow managed to convince myself that we weren't picking up anything because it wasn't set right.

"Scared about what?" Betty questioned with a frown, "The war has ended…what is there to be scared about?"

I sighed and shook my head, "what if the war hasn't ended?"

"I heard the broadcast yesterday…"

"I know, but this has been going on for the last 5 years, would it really have just ended like that?" I stared into my cup and swirled the liquid around before biting the inside of my lip and glancing up at Betty. "I've lost too much to accept that it's over and find out that it isn't, I don't think I can survive much more."

Betty shrugged, "It isn't worth thinking about Rose. They announced it yesterday, it's over today, you don't have to deal with anything anymore."

I sighed again and rested my chin on the table. "But what if it isn't? What if they found something else to fight about and forgot to tell us?" I bit my lip and turned my watery eyes up to Betty. She gave me an amused smile.

"Is this why you've been sat out here for hours?"

I nodded solemnly.

"Have you heard anything indicating otherwise?"

"Well…no…"

Betty laughed, "Exactly. Now relax. Everything is over and we should be out celebrating. I heard rumours of a street party later this evening."

I rubbed the back of my neck and focused my attention on the wireless. Betty slapped my hands away.

"Leave it, otherwise you'll mess something up and then we won't hear if anything has changed."

I looked at her panicked. "Do you think something will have changed?"

She started to shake her head quickly, "Wow, for somebody who seems quite calm and collected, you do panic quickly."

I narrowed my eyes at her.

"No Rose, I don't think anything will change in the next few hours. The war is over. It's done. We're free."

***

I didn't move from my position next to the wireless until I had listened to a broadcast, any broadcast, so it was clear what was happening. It wasn't that I didn't believe Betty, but I was a little uncomfortable about how quickly things had changed. It didn't take long until a loud crackle from my right alerted me to the incoming broadcast. I held my breath in anticipation when I heard Churchill's voice ring out.

"Yesterday morning at 2:41am at Headquarters, General Jodl, the representative of the German High Command..."

I could hear Betty pottering around in her room and immediately screamed for her. "Betty! Churchill is speaking! Something is happening..."

Betty trotted out with a grin but rolled her eyes at me. "Will you believe me if you hear Churchill confirm it then?"

I scowled at her and turned my attention back to the radio as I heard Churchill clear his throat.

"Hostilities will end officially at one minute after midnight tonight, but in the interests of saving lives the cease fire began yesterday to be sounded all along the front, and our dear Channel Islands are also to be freed today."

I screamed again. "It's over! It's over!" I threw my arms around Betty and dragged her around the room in an impromptu dance. She laughed and shook her head.

"You're ridiculous. You do know this, right?"

I nodded and squealed happily. "Of course I do, Mamma used to tell me all the time."

Betty studied my face for a few seconds, I usually got extremely upset after talking about my mother, but for once I didn't. At that particular moment, the fact I'd lost my family didn't matter. I quietened in time to catch the end of Churchill's speech.

"We must now devote all our strength and resources to the completion of our task, both at home and abroad. Advance, Britannia! Long live the cause of freedom! God save the King!"

***

An hour after the broadcast was heard by everybody in England; Betty informed me that they were planning a last minute street party. By the time I forced myself out of the flat, Betty was already in the street running around excitedly.

"It's over!" she screamed and jumped at me. "It's finally over!"

Although I was still torn between being excited or upset, I couldn't help but get caught up in the joy of the atmosphere.

"I know," I gave her a grin, "I can't believe it!"

Several patrons of surrounding pubs had spilled out onto the street, cheering happily and sloshing their drinks all over the place. Betty grabbed my hand and trotted down the street with me in tow. She thrust a pint of something in my hands and ordered me to drink up.

"What the hell is in this?" I hissed and bit back a cough.

"Ask Pat, he just turned up with a massive keg full." Betty shrugged and jerked her head in the direction of Pat. He was stood in the centre of a group of people who seemed to be hanging onto his every word.

I pulled a face when I took another mouthful and quickly handed the glass back to her. Pat appeared by my side and immediately grabbed my wrist. I hadn't even seen him move.

"Get it down ya girly!" He forced the glass to my mouth again and waited until I had unwillingly finished the rest of the drink.

"What *is* in it?" I asked again as I coughed at the burning sensation which was running down my throat.

"A bit of this and that." He replied evasively with a wink before nudging me with his elbow. "There's a lot of whiskey in there though. I seem to remember you enjoying it…"

I rolled my eyes and gave him the glass.

"I call it VE-ry Victorious!"

I snorted, "Catchy."

Pat went to fill my glass up with some more but I quickly declined and hurried away so I wasn't forced to drink the vile mixture any longer. I swallowed a squeak of surprise when I spotted Ma'am dancing with a young boy and laughing wildly. Betty couldn't contain her amusement when she spotted the scene herself.

"Well, Ma'am has finally let her hair down." She giggled and looped her arm through mine. I agreed.

"Literally." I mumbled a while later when I noticed that her snowy grey hair wasn't tied back in its usual bun but was left flowing around her shoulders.

"She looks…" I started and paused to see if I could think of the right word.

"Almost human?" Betty offered which sent us both into peals of laughter. We bit our lips to stop ourselves from noticeably giggling when she looked our way and for a few minutes thought we were going to get reprimanded. Instead, she gave us both a massive smile and waved before carrying on dancing. We looked at each other in shock.

"That was unexpected…" Betty giggled and started to walk down the street again.

"Where are you going?" I called out when she turned around and beckoned me over.

"I heard there was food at the other end of the street, near the tube station." She waited patiently for me to join her.

"They really went all out for this didn't they?" I mused and looked around at the make shift decorations that were hung up around street lights and across garden gates. Light was also filtering through the open doors of the houses that had been left standing and it caused me to panic slightly because of the blackout rule, but I quickly remembered that it didn't matter, not anymore.

"Well it's not every day that we can celebrate the end of the war."

I hummed in agreement and eyed the mountain of food suspiciously.

"How could they afford to do this with the rationing in place?" I questioned in wonder, though I wasn't sure why I'd asked Betty. She shrugged and joined the end of the queue.

"Maybe the government has been lax with the restrictions because it's a day of celebration?"

"Hmmm…I don't think that seems likely."

Betty rolled her eyes. "Who cares? It's here, we're here, lets enjoy!"

***

As darkness fell around us, people from other areas of London started to join in our festivities.

"Why are there so many people coming here?" I asked Betty as we joined in with the massive group of dancing people. She shrugged, grabbed my hand and spun me around.

"I think it has something to do with the fireworks in a little while."

I looked at her with wide eyes, "We have fireworks?!"

"Apparently so, they wanted tonight to be as memorable as possible."

I nodded slowly, "I doubt I'll be forgetting tonight any time soon."

Betty giggled and continued to spin me around as we danced, until they called for the music to stop and shifted us away from the area where they were going to set off the fireworks. I'd never seen fireworks before so I wasn't entirely sure what to expect, but I'd been told by many people that they were quite fun to watch. What I hadn't expected was the constant bangs that came as they exploded in the air and it dredged up some terrible memories, especially as the smoke started to filter through the street.

They sounded very similar to the bombs that we'd experienced raining down on us for 9 months, and it was little distressing. I could feel myself panicking so I grabbed a hold of Betty's hand and squeezed it tight whenever one whizzed off into the darkened sky. Admittedly they were very pretty to watch but it appeared that I wasn't the only one who seemed fairly jumpy at the constant bangs.

"Aren't they pretty?" Betty whispered in awe. She couldn't help but flinch at the noise but seemed to be handling it much better than I was.

"Yeah, they are…" I replied as I watched the colours explode across the sky, lighting up the street briefly as they burst. I could hear a chorus of 'ooh's' and 'aah's' as the fireworks took their shape.

"Kind of fitting don't you think?" Betty mumbled a few minutes later as the last few fireworks were set alight.

"What do you mean?" I shivered and cuddled closer to her. She sighed happily and glanced over at me.

"Well, the war started for us with a series of explosions and bright lights, it just seems fitting that it ends in the same way."

172

I laughed softly and frowned in concern as I spotted one of the fireworks in the middle of the street, smoking profusely. It looked like it was going to explode at any given moment, so we all moved backwards slowly in the thick smoke.

There was a shriek of fear as the firework slid off of its stand and flew through the surrounding people who darted around in all direction to get away from it. I giggled in amusement as I watched the chaos and paid no attention to the series of gasps that Betty was emitting beside me.

"Rose…" Betty called and started to poke me in the arm. I waved her off and continued to watch the running people with wide eyes. I hoped nobody was going to get injured.

"Rose…" she called again, her voice held more urgency. I frowned and turned to face her when she started to shake my shoulder.

"What is it?" I asked quickly when I looked at the face she was pulling. She pointed towards an area thick with smoke and the shadowy figure that was walking towards us.

"Is that…?" she asked slowly, I turned my attention to the figure and my heart leapt into my throat.

"It can't be…" I whispered and shook my head in disbelief. Betty hooked her arm through mine and held me tight to her side.

"I think it is…" she answered just as quietly. I continued to start at the emerging figure. "I hope so…"

It felt as if time had completely slowed down as the figure walked through the thick layer of smoke and with each step they took, the tighter my chest became and the more hopeful I became.

"Rose, go to him…"

I shook my head, "I can't. What if it isn't him?"

Betty pushed me forward slightly, "You're not going to know if you don't walk over there. It can't hurt to see?"

I sighed and stumbled forward a few more steps. I strained my eyes to see if I could make out anything more on the figure that seemed so familiar to me. The world seemed to slow even more as we walked towards each other and I swear I stopped breathing when I heard a broken voice call out my name.

"Ro-se?"

It was Edward. He had finally come back home to me. I broke out into a run and threw myself at him, quickly wrapping my arms around his neck and my legs around his waist, peppering kisses all over his face.

"I've missed you! So much!" I sobbed and held tightly onto him. It felt amazing to have him back in my arms again, I'd missed the contact more than I had realised.

"I've missed you too my darling." Edward nuzzled his head into my neck and pressed a series of small kisses to the skin he could reach.

"You're home?" I questioned though the answer was obvious, I just needed to hear him clarify it.

"I'm home…" He untangled my legs from behind him and set me down on the floor, he continued to clutch me to him in a tight hug however.

"For good?" I whispered, terrified that he would have to go back and fight elsewhere. I knew the war was over in Europe but there were still hostilities between America and Japan.

"For good…" He stepped back and glanced down at his bags.

"I'm not going anywhere without you." He held my face between his cold hands and kissed my nose before bringing his lips to my mouth and pressing a soft, tender kiss to them. "Ever."

I started giggling happily and quickly waved Betty over. "It's Edward!" I exclaimed with a massive grin and tears streaming down my face, although she could clearly see who it was. "He's come home!" I clapped my hands together in glee. Betty and Edward quickly said hello before they turned their attention back to me.

"I can't believe you're here." I whispered with wide eyes. "I can't believe you made it back."

Edward laughed and pecked the tip of my nose. "I told you that I'd never say goodbye."

***

Chapter Nineteen

Present Day

I looked around the room at the people I loved and smiled. It hadn't been as hard as I thought it would be to re-tell the story of my past.

"You're incredible Nanna…" Suzie wiped the tears from her eyes and kissed my forehead. "I'm honoured that you shared that part of your life with us, it must have been difficult."

I winked at her and laughed, "So it wasn't just an old ladies memory then?"

Suzie shook her head vigorously. "No! It was an amazing story. I'd be blessed if you let me write about it…"

"Ah, little Suzie, our budding writer." I gave her a warm smile and nodded. "If you can make it sound much better than my hazy memories then you're more than welcome darling."

She squealed and jumped off of the bed so she could wind her arms around my neck. I winced at the pain that shot through my body but made sure she didn't notice I was hurting. I gave her a tight hug back and swallowed around the tears that were gathering in my throat. I was such an emotional wreck.

I started at the back wall of the room to try and calm myself down and noticed that we were one person down in the room.

"Where did Trent go?" I must have been extremely involved in the telling of my story to not notice the 6'4" boy leave.

"Don't you worry Ma, he had to pick something up. He'll be back soon." Elsie smiled, I nodded with a frown.

"Did he say where he was going?"

Nobody answered me and for some reason it concerned me. I wasn't the type of person who needed to know what everyone was doing at every given minute of the day, but I was prone to worry when somebody just left without telling me first. Though, it appeared I needn't have worried given he appeared at the door mere minutes later, with a sheepish grin.

"Nanna, I have something for you."

I waited quietly to see what he was going to do next.

"Rose! Why didn't you tell me you were in here? I've been worried sick, which at my age isn't the greatest idea." Betty hobbled out from behind Trent and zeroed in on me with a massive grin. I squealed in happiness.

"I was rushed out! I couldn't tell you!" I held my hand out for my friend as she made her way over. Elsie quickly jumped out of her seat.

"Albert thinks I'm crazy." Betty huffed and plopped down into the seat, pushing her thick red rimmed glasses back up her face. They clashed terribly with her purple rinse hair but I wasn't going to say anything.

"Why does Albert think you're crazy?" I asked slowly. Albert was one of the residents at the care home that she'd had her eyes on for ages. At first he was a little unhappy with her advances since he'd just lost his wife, but he was slowly coming round to her pestering.

"He thought you were just in your room being grouchy. He didn't believe me when I told him that something was wrong."

I laughed softly, "how long have you been telling him that I wasn't there then?"

She frowned for a second and stuck her bottom lip out as her teeth fell down. Her denture glue wasn't strong enough but she wasn't going to ask for anything stronger. She hated the teeth as it was.

"I don't remember, but it wasn't until this strapping young lad came in to get me that he believed me." She looked up at Trent and squinted. "He looks so much like your Edward back in the war." She mused and then nodded her head. "Yes, very much like your Edward."

I giggled and agreed with her. "I know, it's surprising really."

Betty turned her attention back to me and raised a wrinkled hand to my face. "You're not leaving me are you?" She muttered sadly and clicked her teeth back into place before they fell down as she was talking. It happened quite often and was amusing for the rest of us.

"I'm not planning on it!" I gave her a grin and patted her on the hand. "I've still got a lot of fight left in me."

Betty peered at me through her glasses. I couldn't help but laugh because her eyes were incredibly magnified by the outside of them and it made her look quite comical.

"Good." She huffed and crossed her arms. "You promised me you'd never leave."

I laughed, "Betty, that was over 60 years ago."

She narrowed her eyes at me. "It doesn't matter *when* it was. You still promised."

I smiled at her and sighed, "You have Albert to keep you company now."

She immediately pulled a face and scowled. "Albert isn't interested. He made that evident."

"How? What did he do?"

"He bought me some carnations. He knows I don't like carnations – my favourite flower is a lily!" Betty huffed and crossed her arms as she leant back into the chair that pretty much swallowed up her small frame.

"Have you ever told him that...?"

"Well, not in so many words."

I rolled my eyes and giggled. "Then it's hardly a surprise really is it? He likes you Betty, you've been pestering him for so long that he's finally responding to it."

I found it amusing that even at 88 I was still giving my best friend relationship advice.

Somebody cleared their throat from across the room and as I turned to look, I immediately remembered that we were in the room with my family.

"Oh!" I blushed and rubbed my forehead in embarrassment. "Sorry, I forgot you were here..."

My two daughters immediately feigned hurt, I smiled apologetically.

"Betty." I looked over at her and suppressed a snort when I'd noticed she'd fallen asleep. "Betty!" I poked her in the arm and waited for her to open her eyes. When she finally looked at me blearily, I introduced her to the rest of my family.

"Everybody, this is Betty. Betty, this is my family." I knew there was no point in naming each and every single one of them - she had a tendency to forget something as soon as she'd been told it.

"Nanna, why have we not met Betty before?" Isaac asked what appeared to be something the rest of the room was thinking. I shrugged.

"Every time you came to visit she'd be off gallivanting with her latest conquest."

Betty hit me on the side of my arm. "I was not!"

I put my hand up to the side of my mouth and mock whispered. "Don't listen to her, she's crazy."

Betty made a noise of disagreement which caused the room to burst out laughing. She started sulking in the corner.

"I've never seen you like this before Ma." Elsie hummed, my other daughter nodded in agreement.

"What do you mean?" I rested my head against the pillow and shut my eyes for a few seconds as a wave of nausea and dizziness passed.

"I just mean that you seem really carefree and joyful."

I shrugged, "Betty usually brings that side out of me. She's frequently told me that I worry too much and I was going to work myself into an early grave."

"I have told her that!" Betty chirped from her chair. I threw her a smile.

"If it wasn't for her, then I doubt I would have gotten through the war."

Betty blushed and reached out for my hand. "I agree. You probably wouldn't have done." She stuck her tongue out and fought back a yawn.

"When are you coming home, Rose?"

I frowned and shrugged again, "I don't know, the doctors aren't sure what's happening yet."

"Oh, well I hope it's soon. It's far too quiet without you around."

There were a few short minutes of silence before Betty cleared her throat and groaned as she tried to stand up from her chair.

Trent immediately ran over to help her and with a grateful smile she made her way over to her bag by the door.

"Rose, I have something for you." She grinned at me and waited for Trent to hand her the bag so she could go through it. She returned a few minutes later with a black box and handed it to me.

"I found these in your room and thought you could probably use them close by." She grinned at me.

I opened the box and looked down at its contents. Inside was a photograph of my mother and two younger brothers, every letter Edward had ever sent me, scraps of memories throughout my life and nestled on top were my two medals.

"How did you find this?" I asked with a whisper. Betty frowned,

"What was that about a fish?" She asked. I snorted and repeated myself louder.

"I said, how did you find this?"

"Albert helped me find the stuff in your room; he got one of his sons to bring the box in."

"Thank you!" I all but shouted.

"What is it ma?" Elsie asked, I turned the box to show them and sat back as it was passed around.

***

Once I had the box in my hands again, I glanced around the room and was surprised by the fact that most of its occupants, including my nurse Susan, were crying.

"Why the tears?" I hadn't said anything for a while so there was no reason that I could think of for the tears.

"It's because of the letters Rose." Betty mumbled from my side, her eyes were also red-rimmed.

"What do you mean 'it's the letters'?" I asked my best friend. She shook her head incredulously.

"They are so heartfelt, so loving and I remember everything that you went through quite clearly. I didn't realise that you spoke to Edward as much as you did…"

The younger children in the room didn't understand what was going on, but seemed a little concerned that the majority of the room were weeping. I sighed and bit my lip. "None of that matters anymore. I've had the happy ending I've always wanted."

They all watched me as waited for me to carry on talking.

"I was blessed with a wonderful husband, two wonderful daughters and seven grandchildren. I wouldn't have changed anything for the world."

The tears continued streaming down the faces of everybody.

"I miss dad." Betty cried from my right, I turned to face her slowly.

"I know darling, I miss him too. He's always here though." I placed my hand over her heart. "And I will be too, when I go."

"Ma, don't say that!" Elsie cried from my left. I smiled sadly at the both of them.

"I know it's horrible to think about darlings, but it's true. The doctors aren't sure I'm going to get through this one." This fact terrified me beyond belief and I hated that it was true. The nurse cleared her throat and made her way over to the bed.

"Don't talk like that Rose, you're a fighter, you'll get through this." She smiled and handed me my cocktail of pain relievers. Not that they were doing much, I was still in agony.

"Sometimes you just have to accept what is coming your way girls, and this is it for me I'm afraid." I mumbled with a shrug and then took the water from Susan and swallowed my pills. My grandchildren all looked at me broken heartedly. "Grammy, please don't say that!"

I smiled at them and laughed a little, "Don't you worry, I'll be watching over everybody and I'll haunt you if you're naughty!"

"Mother! Will you stop saying these things please? You're upsetting everyone and you know that you'll be fine in a couple of days." Betty admonished and then hugged her youngest who had started to sob.

I sighed and leaned back into the pillows, allowing my eyes to drift shut. I was so tried all the time and it was made worse by talking quite a lot. With a sad smile I asked everybody to leave.

"If you don't mind, I think I'd quite like a nap now. Telling you about the war always tires me out…" I explained through my tiredness, "Come back in a few hours, I'll be ready to talk more then." I felt everybody kiss me goodbye and then relaxed even more when the door shut. I jumped slightly when I heard somebody clear their throat beside me.

"You're not getting rid of me that easy." My friend croaked, she pulled her knitting out of her bag. "I'm not leaving the room, I hate being at the care home without you, I'd rather stay with you."

I nodded slowly, "That's fine, but forgive me if I fall asleep…"

She smiled at me and brought her knitting right up to her eyes so she could see what she was doing. "I'll be quiet as a mouse. You won't even know I'm here."

I sighed, rested my head back against the pillow and thought about the day. I hated upsetting everyone, but they needed to realise that I wasn't going to be around forever. In fact, I doubted I'd be around for much longer.

I let my thoughts drift back to the husband I'd lost and the life I had been living before I'd gotten bed ridden by the illness. It wasn't much of a life admittedly but I'd been happy playing checkers with Betty at the care home every Friday when she decided she wasn't going to try and pursue Albert. She was 89 years old but still as feisty as she had been at 20. I had meant to tell her that he had been looking for her the day I'd gotten taken into hospital but I'd forgotten by the time I'd seen her. I seemed to be forgetting a lot these days, I didn't remember where I'd put my slippers, or my books. Nor did I seem to remember what day of the week it was or even what year it was anymore. Though, the one thing I never forgot was my husband. My beautiful, wonderful husband with whom I'd been married to for nearly 60 years but he'd died just before our anniversary in a peaceful sleep when I was merely 79.

We finally remarried in the summer of 1948, when we could afford to pay for it. He looked different to how he was when I first met him; he was much more withdrawn and spent a lot of time just staring out into the distance without talking for hours. None of that mattered though because he was back with me, back where he was supposed to be. Our wedding was a small and very quiet affair. His family didn't bother coming over from Canada, they didn't care about me because I'd 'taken him away from them', but a couple of soldiers that he'd served with did turn up. Betty, Pat and Ma'am were on my side at the wedding, but that was it.

Elizabeth Joan McGraw was born 9 months later, on March 10th 1949, at a small 5lbs 5oz. She was a breath of fresh air and reignited mine and Edward's relationship. We moved to the countryside a few months later. Elsie Margaret McGraw was born nearly exactly 9 months later on December 23rd 1949, on the 10th anniversary of the dance that bought Edward to me. She very swiftly let us know that she was going to be a bundle of mischief. Edward and I joked that she was the reason that we both started going grey before we were 40.

Edward and I visited Canada a few times over the span of our marriage and his family grew to like me. We were there for his first niece being born and we were there the night his father passed away.

The Home Guard was stood down at the end of the war, so I spent a lot of my early 30s at home with the children, it wasn't until the 60s/70s that I ventured out to get a job, it wasn't anything amazing but it helped bring in extra money that was needed. In the 80s we both renewed our vows in a much larger ceremony than our wedding. Elsie and Betty had planned everything and it was given as a surprise for our 40th wedding anniversary. It was during the 80s that Betty fell pregnant with her first daughter, our first grandchild and she didn't stop popping them out from then. Here I was, in 2009, one daughter with 5 children, the other with 2. Both married to strapping lads that I knew would take care of them when I was gone and here I was left, lying alone, in a hospital bed.

"Rosie?"

My eyes shot open when I heard a voice I'd not heard for years. Immediately I saw Edward standing next to my bedside, in a Soldier's uniform that I hadn't seen him wear since we were 40 and he was dressing up for our annual fancy dress new years party.

"Edward?" I don't know why I questioned it, I knew who he was - I'd never forget who he was.

"Oh Rosie, how I've missed you so!" He reached his hand out and stroked my cheek. I was startled that I could feel his touch for a brief second but relaxed and leaned into it soon after.

"I've missed you too my darling. I've missed you so much." I covered his hand with mine and took a deep breath the calm my tears.

"I've been with you every day I've been gone my love, I never left your side." He whispered and pressed a soft kiss to my forehead. I gave him a watery smile.

"Why did you leave me?" I whispered and winced in agony as a cough started hacking through my body. Edward immediately pressed his hand against my chest and the coughing ceased, the pain immediately disappeared.

"It was just my time to go." He smiled sadly, "I'm here now though."

I watched him silently for a few minutes as realisation dawned on me. He stepped away from the bed and held out his hand. "Dance with me Rosie."

"There's no music..." I whispered. He quickly waved his hand at me and before I could understand what was going on I could hear music playing. It was the first ever song we danced to way back in 1939.

"Come on sweetheart, for old time's sake?"

I sat up slowly expecting my body to groan in protest but was pleasantly surprised to find that I felt no pain or any stiffness; instead I was able to move like I was 18 again. I trotted over to him and wrapped my arms around his middle, breathing in the smell that I'd missed for the past 10 years.

He held me tight to him and started to sway around the room to the music whilst he hummed along with it. He had always hummed, whistled or sung along to any music he knew. When he was still alive and pottering around in the garden or in his den, I'd hear his lovely voice float through the house. I'd missed it terribly when he'd gone.

"I love you Rosie. I've wanted to tell you every day, I just didn't have chance." He smiled and kissed my hair.

"I love you too Edward." I mumbled against his shirt and my body immediately felt at peace. I wasn't scared or worried that I was talking to my dead husband, let alone could feel him pressed up against me. I was just happy to be back where I belonged. There was a short comfortable silence between us again.

"Forgive me for being forward, but you're incredibly beautiful."
He mumbled with a small laugh. I grinned up at him and winked.
"You'll never be too forward."

The music tapered off and I sighed, I knew what was coming
next and for the first time in my life, I was ready. I'd said
goodbye to my children, I'd seen my grandchildren one last time
and now it was time for me to leave them and let them continue
with their own lives and create their own stories.

"Come on Rosie, it's time." Edward smiled at me and held out
his hand. I clasped it tightly and smiled at him.

"There's nothing to be scared of darling, everything will be fine."
He kissed the back of my head and led me towards the door. I
took one last look behind me and saw my 88 year old body lying
on the bed with a blissful smile on her face before I left the room
and my life behind me.

****

Epilogue

I looked down on my best friend as she took her final breath. I hadn't wanted to leave her side because, for some reason, I could tell that she was beginning to leave us. Her face had started to turn grey, her breaths were becoming laboured and she seemed extremely tired all of a sudden. I watched a smile appear on her face moments before she passed away and shed a little tear for the life she had just left. She was a wonderful person and I was honoured that I had the chance to be her best friend for the majority of our lives. If I hadn't jumped at her when I saw her walk in to the school hall, many decades earlier, then I would have missed out on the sweetest and kindest friend anybody could've asked for. Although she'd left me and finally had broken her promise, I was happy enough to know that she'd gone back to Edward and was where she belonged – in Heaven.

I rested my knitting on my knee and leant back in the chair, sighing in sadness. I didn't want to tell the doctors that she had passed, since I wanted to be alone with my thoughts for a while, but I felt a little guilty since her family should've known already. Part of me wondered if she'd asked everybody to leave because she felt that it was time to go and her family didn't need to see that. It wouldn't surprise me, it was something that Rose would do. She was ever thoughtful about the people around her, they always came first, even if it was at her own expense. It was one of the greatest things about her, her selflessness, it even awarded her medals.

My thoughts swiftly drifted back to that day, a couple of months after the war had ended, when the government had sorted out the relevant paperwork. It turned out to be a beautiful day, even if Rose was adamant that she didn't deserve the medals.

***

1945

"I don't deserve these!" Rose hissed as I tugged at the collar of her jacket and straightened her hat so it was pinned onto her hair at an angle. "I don't understand why they're awarding me these."

Edward stood up from the chair in the corner of the room and quickly made his way over, pecking his wife on her lips.

"Because, my darling Rose, you're incredible."

She blushed and looked up at me for reassurance.

"Rose who else did as much as you in the war effort?" I asked quietly. She shrugged and started to fiddle with the brooch on her lapel.

"Probably a lot that we don't know about..." She stared at herself in the mirror one last time and then turned back to us with a huff.

"Then they will get the recognition that they deserve. This is yours Rose, enjoy it."

We were currently in one of the empty rooms in the Town Hall, where the ceremony was taking place. Rose had been waiting outside but a case of nerves had overtaken her when she'd seen that there were quite a lot of people sat outside waiting for the ceremony to start. She wasn't the only one receiving a medal but she did have a rather large group of people there to support her. She flapped her hands around in nervousness and started to pace. I grabbed her wrists.

"Rose, calm down! Seriously, there is nothing to get uptight about. This is a celebration…"

She nodded slowly, "I know, I just…this isn't…this is my idea of hell."

I laughed softly at the same time Edward chuckled.

"We know." We both told her in unison. She hadn't stopped telling us how uncomfortable the whole thing was making her.

"Look, all you're going to have to do is walk up there with a big smile on your face, accept the medals, salute and then stand off to the side…"

She looked a little green at the thought of it all. "What if I forget my name? Or stumble? Or I don't salute correctly?" She muttered quickly and went to drag her hand through her hair. I quickly slapped it away.

"Darling, you'll be perfect." Edward paused and then peered out into the hall. "I think it's time for you to go out there Rosie, we'll be sat at the front." He wrapped his arms around her in another reassuring hug. "I love you."

***

I wasn't sure who the people were that were on the stage talking to us, aside from the Prime Minister himself, but there was a lengthy speech before anybody was allowed to be given their honours. Both Edward and I waited with baited breath as Rose walked up to the podium and her story was told to the hall. A hush fell among the audience as they listen to what she was put through, through the 6 years of the war. They then erupted into a very loud, very heartfelt round of applause after the speaker had finished. She turned towards us, bowed and proudly showed off her George Cross and her Royal Red Cross.

The second the ceremony was over, Rose bounded down the stairs and towards us with a huge grin on her face.

"Look!" She squealed, pulling her jacket out so we could get a closer look at them.

"Look at them!" she giggled.

***

2009

I smiled at the memory of her joy that had stayed with her for days afterwards before turning my attention back to her lifeless body on the bed in front of me. I leant forward and kissed her forehead in goodbye.

"Sleep well Rose. I'll see you soon."

****

THE END